Ghostly Theatre

The Merrie Devil

Maureen Spurgeon

An Armada Original

For
The Allwork Drama Workshop

The Merrie Devil was first published in the UK
in Armada in 1989

Armada is an imprint of the Children's Division,
part of the Collins Publishing Group,
8 Grafton Street, London W1X 3LA

Printed and bound in Great Britain by
William Collins Sons & Co. Ltd, Glasgow

One

"You know," said Oliver, absent-mindedly kicking at a stubby clump of grass, "you'd never think Lynsey was that old. I mean — nearly twenty one!"

"You make her sound ancient!" Rachel objected, tossing her head back so that her long fair hair caught the light of the pale April sunshine. "Mum was only twenty one when I was born, and seeing that I'm twelve this year, the same as you — "

"Oh, you know what I'm getting at!" Oliver interrupted impatiently. "Look at the way she was working on that sword fight routine with us last week, wearing those pink dungaree things and her hair tied in bunches. Anyone would have thought she was one of us, instead of someone actually running her own drama workshop!"

"Anyway," Jason's deep voice broke in before Rachel had the chance to answer back, "how did we get on the subject of how old Lynsey was?"

Oliver and Rachel grinned at each other. Jason had a reputation for being a real day-dreamer.

"Because," explained Oliver, studying his own round face and brown curls in Jason's steel-rimmed glasses, "Lynsey's twenty first birthday is the same weekend as this Anniversary Pageant everyone's talking about. You know, when Dreyton celebrates being six hundred years old."

"Oh," Jason nodded slowly. "That . . ." He peered around at the deserted churchyard where they sat, huddled together on a low stone wall. "D'you reckon she's going to be long?"

"Lynsey?" enquired Scott. "She only went into the hall a

few minutes ago. Tina's signing on today, so there's the membership form and stuff to sort out, voice test and everything, but it shouldn't last too long. Lynsey couldn't fit it in after last Saturday's workshop, because it was the Mayor's Charity Bring and Buy Sale in the afternoon. Trust me to get roped in, helping one of my teachers from St Helena's Academy!"

Oliver glanced at his watch, bleeping in time with the chimes of the town clock in the distance.

"We'd better get going," he said, and slid off the wall, dusting down the seat of his track suit trousers. He thrust his hands deep into his pockets and led the way through a line of parked cars towards the Parish Hall.

"We should find out about *The Merrie Devil of Dreyton* today," said Oliver. "Lynsey said she'd be looking into it for us!"

"Yes," said Rachel. This anniversary pageant is only a few months away, isn't it? We ought to be getting started on something by now."

"Not much good if this *Merrie Devil of Dreyton* doesn't turn out to be the sort of production we can do, though," Jason pointed out. "Might not have anything to do with this Dreyton, for a start!"

"Of course it's to do with this Dreyton!" Rachel flared up. "Lynsey said that, as soon as I showed her that piece I copied from one of Daddy's old theatre annuals. And *he's* sure it must be this Dreyton, because he and mum have even wondered about their Stagecoach Group producing it. Why d'you think he remembered it in the first place?"

"OK, OK!" Jason grinned good naturedly. "I was only wondering about it as well, the same as them."

"Be good if we could do it, though," added Oliver. "The Studio Workshop presents – *The Merrie Devil of Dreyton*.

Sounds great, doesn't it? All about monsters, and ghosts and demons, with loads of scary sound effects!"

They marched up the gravel path to the heavy oak door of the Parish Hall.

Oliver wondered why so much noise was coming from the hall. Drama workshops were never quiet affairs, what with voice work, crowd scenes, stage fights and so on — but there was generally more of a hum in the breaks between sessions. This time though, he could hear a buzz of chatter and laughter above the music from the ancient tape recorder, even a sprinkling of applause.

"Take it easy ... Keep those feet and hands nice and steady," came Lynsey's clear voice, as he pushed the door open. "You lot are exactly five minutes late!" she continued, without taking her eyes off the small girl dancing around the hall, looking so much like Scott that it could only be his sister.

Jason opened his mouth to protest, but Lynsey was already stepping towards the middle of the floor.

"Don't forget to move your head, Tina," she instructed, demonstrating in a trail of blue ribbon. "Otherwise the leg and arm movements will look odd."

"Thought you said your sister was shy, Scotty," accused Oliver. Tina's small arms and legs, knees and elbows were still moving in such perfect rhythm, he could almost see the puppet strings being pulled.

One or two of the girls knew Tina as the latest recruit to the gym club at Dreyton Comprehensive, where she had joined Scott last term, so they had an idea what to expect. Everyone else was just as surprised as Oliver.

"I wasn't the one who said she was shy," Scott sounded indignant. "That's only what my mum's always saying."

Even Rachel was enthusiastic, yelling out: "Brilliant!" before she could stop herself, and leading a fresh burst of applause which probably would have gone on for quite a while, if Lynsey hadn't given one or two sharp claps herself.

"Well done, Tina!" she cried, raising her voice above the last few notes of music. "I really think we could use that as a warm-up routine for the others to try."

Scott was embarrassed to see that Tina was actually blushing bright red, turning her head away and looking down at her hands, twisting them this way and that. He was glad that nobody else seemed to notice.

"Quiet, everyone!" Lynsey clapped her hands again, green eyes glaring at one or two persistent talkers near the back. "I want to talk about the Dreyton Anniversary celebrations, and what the Studio Workshop hopes to be doing!"

"This is us, Ollie!" Rachel murmured, her face glowing expectantly.

"Now we haven't worked out anything definite, not yet. So I want you to start thinking up some ideas about how we could present something from the town's history! You can work on a mime of the work which Dreyton people used to do," Lynsey went on, ignoring a sharp hiss of breath from Rachel, "or maybe act out a visit by somebody famous – anything you like! See what you can do, and we'll go through everything towards the end of the morning."

"But ... but – " Rachel stammered, "what about my *Merrie Devil of Dreyton*? You promised you'd see if we could do it, Lynsey!"

"I said I'd try and find out about it, Rachel!" Lynsey corrected. "And the fact is that nobody seems to have heard anything about it, not even the committee organizing the anniversary celebrations. It doesn't look as if it's quite so important as you thought!"

"Oh, Lynsey – " Oliver looked so dejected that Lynsey patted his shoulder.

8

"Don't worry, we haven't quite given up! Peter Albany-Smith has been judging the Drama Festival at Picking all week, so I'll be seeing him at the award ceremony tonight. He might come up with some clues."

"Peter Albany-Smith!" groaned Oliver, remembering the carefully trimmed beard, the floppy bow ties, the cufflinks, gold watches and bracelets winking out from rows of frills and lace. "He never seems to know what's going on right under his nose, never mind something that happened hundreds of years ago!"

"Oh, he's not that bad! People say he'd have made a good actor if he hadn't gone into managing theatrical companies and raising cash to put shows on the road!"

"Peter Albany-Smith," echoed Scott, with a look of horror on his face. "We could do the scripts, sort out the props *and* paint the scenery while he's dithering around!"

"We'll get told off for dithering around if we don't look out!" said Oliver. "Lynsey's already got her eye on us!"

"Well, I'm not doing any mimes of jobs or visits by famous people!" said Rachel flatly, arms folded with grim determination.

"Why don't we do our own story on this *Merrie Devil of Dreyton*?" Oliver suggested, seizing on the first idea which came into his head.

"Great idea!" said Rachel. "We'll start off with you being the writer, Ollie, holding a quill pen and a candlestick and all that! And," she added, impulsively grabbing Tina's small hand, "let's try Scotty's sister as the page or the servant, or somebody!"

One thing about Rachel, Jason considered, she was never down for very long. Seeing her beginning to flounce around in an imaginary gown and veil, it was quite a shock to remember the drooping shoulders and the glum mouth of only a few moments before.

"Hey!" cut in Oliver. "Are you with us Jason? That's the third time we've said you're going to be the squire, coming to see about this Merrie Devil I've been writing about, because the tale is frightening everyone! Right?"

"Right!" agreed Jason, coming down to earth with one of his crooked grins. "What about Scott?"

"Can't you guess?" giggled Tina. "He's the Merrie Devil!"

They were all pleased to see how quick Tina was to get into her part, using so many cheeky expressions and comical movements that it seemed quite natural to think of the writer's servant being able to conjure up the Merrie Devil, with Rachel as the poor wife being tormented by their magic and calling on the brave squire for help.

Lynsey was most impressed.

"That's the way to work an imaginary theme into a true-life situation!" she told them approvingly. "Think you could do a bit more work on this idea before next Saturday's workshop?"

"We don't mind," said Rachel firmly, "as long as *you* don't forget to tackle Albany-Smith!" Lynsey had to laugh.

But Oliver was more thoughtful, a distant gleam in his brown eyes which Jason knew meant his mind was racing ahead, a long way from a draughty hall with the traffic speeding past outside.

"You know," he said at last, as they edged their way through the crowds of Saturday shoppers, "maybe we should go and look round Dreyton Manor. At least we'd see what the scenery would be like, maybe get some help on props and bits for the script!"

"What's there to see?" demanded Scott. "All the windows and doors are boarded up and padlocked, and there's nothing else except grass and weeds and muck all over the place. I should know. Our football team has to go right past it to get to the new sports stadium."

"Oh, let's go, anyway!" said Jason. "I can't make it till tomorrow afternoon, worse luck. My mum says there's loads of stuff to be sorted out before we go back to Greenlands next week!"

"Don't remind me!" groaned Oliver, who went to the same boys' school as Jason. "What about you, Rachel? Suppose I meet you at the clock tower, somewhere around half past two?"

"Suits me!" said Rachel cheerfully. "Then we can call for Scott and Tina on the way!"

It was no use arguing, Scott realized with a pang, recalling the view of the manor house from his bedroom window, a black, gloomy shape, even without the lights reflected from the motorway.

He remembered frightening Tina when she was little, telling her it was a giant black beetle being squashed against the sky. That was until he saw the moonlight glinting on the broken towers, making them look like long, jagged fingernails clawing desperately for the stars, the windows seeming to stare blindly at him.

It gave him quite a jolt to discover how clear the memory still was.

"Dreyton Manor?" shouted his dad above the whirr of the lawnmower, when Scott raised the subject a bit later on. "What's so special about that old dump, all of a sudden?" he continued after switching the mower off. "Tina was nagging your mum to stop at the library, just to see if there were any photos of the place."

"What?" Scott couldn't wait for her to get back.

"Got anything on Dreyton Manor, Tina?" he burst out as soon as she came through the door. "What did they say at the library?"

"Nothing much, only showed me two postcards, ten pence each. They're in Mum's shopping bag!"

11

She pulled off her gloves and started rummaging through a brown holdall, trying to wriggle out of her anorak at the same time.

"Oh, no you don't!" scolded Mum, stuffing most of the carrier bags into Tina's arms. "I'll give him the postcards, and you can go upstairs and hang up your new clothes before they get creased. Go on!"

"This Dreyton Manor," she went on, rummaging furiously. "You and Tina hardly spoke about the old ruin till she started at drama club this morning."

One glance at the photographs told Scott that he had seen them somewhere before. At the library, probably. And yet – there was so much he seemed to be looking at for the first time.

The tall, thin towers at either side, stretching up to the sky. The magnificent balcony with its huge stone vases, high above an enormous porch lined with pillars. The imposing double doors which stood half open, as though someone was about to call.

Either that, Scott thought again, or as if someone else might be standing on the other side of the door, waiting in the shadows ...

"'Course, it was that fire some years back that finally put an end to the place," his dad was saying. "I wouldn't fancy the rebuilding job, I can tell you."

"Dreyton Manor, 1905," Scott read aloud from the back of one postcard. "Home of the Melrose family until 1920 – "

"Oh, what is that girl doing up there?" Mum broke in impatiently, raising her eyes towards the ceiling. "I've already told her to wait until after tea before she tries everything on!"

"You sit down and have some tea, Joyce," ordered Dad, placing a second mug on the table. "Scott, you go and see what's keeping Tina."

"All right, Dad ... " Somehow, Scott just couldn't take his eyes off the photographs, it was as if there was something missing, something he expected to see.

"Tina," he called softly, and gave a little tap on her bedroom door. There was no answer.

The whole house suddenly seemed so still, so quiet, that he almost began to panic, sighing with relief when the door opened.

Tina was standing there, gazing out of the window, with one hand resting against her silky auburn fringe to shield her eyes from the slanting rays of the sun.

"Tina?"

"Scott ... " Even her voice sounded strange. "Scott, come and look over here. Can you see it?"

"See what? Tina, what are you on about?"

"Th-that horse ... " Scott followed the direction of her pointing finger, trembling just a little. "The golden horse, right at the top of Dreyton Manor."

Two

There was no possible mistake.

Scott could see the proud, sleek head gleaming in the sunshine, casting such a sheen on the broad back, it was as if the horse had just been brushed and groomed. The front hooves pawed at the sky. A thick, curling tail swept behind the strong rear legs, seeming to swish a little against the wind.

"Scott?" Tina had to repeat his name two or three times before he even heard her. "Scott, what's happening?"

Already, the dazzling brightness of the splendid head had softened to a mellow glow which moved slowly along the mane and down the tail, before dissolving into a cold, stony-looking greyness until the horse was nothing more than a still shape outlined against the sky.

"So, it was only the sun," said Tina sadly. "And I really thought it was a golden horse."

"I had a feeling there was something missing from these postcards," said Scott at last, flipping them against his fingers and still staring out of the window. "The camera couldn't get it in, probably."

"Hey, you two!" Dad bawled up the stairs. "How much longer are you going to be?"

Scott and Tina glanced uneasily at each other. Then Tina darted towards the door.

"Just coming, Dad!" she called.

Scott did wonder if she would mention anything about Dreyton Manor or the golden horse, and decided that she probably wouldn't. The whole thing sounded crazy when he thought about it later. But he couldn't wait to

14

investigate Dreyton Manor. Maybe it wouldn't be such a waste of a Sunday afternoon after all.

It was plain that Oliver's idea had grown on Jason as well. Scott noticed his big green eyes sparkling behind the thick spectacles when he opened the front door to find him and Rachel on the doorstep next day.

He was waving a couple of familiar-looking photographs. "The librarian said it was the second lot of Dreyton Manor postcards he'd sold in an hour," he gabbled as they began hurrying along. "When he said it was a ginger-haired kid, I thought it must be you, Scotty!"

"A ginger-haired kid!" Scott almost choked. "I'm no ginger-haired kid! That was Tina!"

"Thanks, Scott," Tina snapped at him. "Now tell Jason about the golden horse."

"Golden horse?" Rachel pricked up her ears. "What golden horse?"

"There isn't one," Scott admitted, rather sheepishly. "Well ... not really, there isn't. Only, yesterday evening, when the sun was shining down on the horse – the one at the top of Dreyton Manor – it looked a bit like gold for a few minutes, that's all."

Tina began to wonder if it really had been like that. The way Scott spoke, there had been nothing special, nothing magical about the long fingers of sunlight stroking a grey stone horse into a proud, golden glory, ready to gallop across the heavens. But she knew she had seen it, and she really thought Scott has seen it, too.

"There's Ollie!" shouted Rachel, as the clock tower came in sight. "That red jacket of his sticks out a mile, doesn't it? Hi, Ollie! Been waiting long?"

"Just got here!" Oliver yelled back. "Wait till you see what I managed to get from the library!"

"Er, you needn't bother to go into details," Jason chipped in, with a sidelong glance at Tina. But Oliver was already unzipping lots of pockets and delving deep inside.

"Soon as the guy started on about someone else asking for info on Dreyton Manor and two kids buying picture postcards, I guessed he meant you lot! So I bought a print of an old map of the Dreyton Estate, and grabbed some free handouts on the anniversary celebrations! Want to see?"

"Nobody can say you waste any time, Ollie," Rachel laughed, whilst the others were still getting their breath back. "Come on, let's head for cover first. I think it's going to rain!"

Sure enough, the deserted pavements were already becoming specked with ominous black spots, enough to make Oliver stuff the wad of papers back inside his jacket as they started to run towards the manor, heads bent against the wind.

The rain was still only a soft drizzle, yet the whole place looked sodden, bedraggled, wearily hunching its once-splendid towers and balconies against the cold.

Tina couldn't help feeling bitterly disappointed. The thick grey walls had seemed so firm and strong from her bedroom window. Now, she could see all too clearly the great, ugly slabs of plywood, held fast by rusty nails, where doors and windows had once looked out onto the well-kept gardens and lawns in the photographs. Great, tooth-edged holes gaped in the brickwork, and even from where she was standing, there was no mistaking the thick streaks of grime and dirt ingrained into the stone pillars. Only the horse rearing up from the topmost gable still raised its magnificent head with pride, waiting to chase the ribbons of cloud being blown across the skies.

"Wonder what's the best way of getting in?" Oliver was saying, standing back a little to get a better view of the

16

wooden hoarding which fenced off the bottom half of the building.

"There's been a bit of patching-up, just here!" called Jason. He and Scott were already beginning to explore. "What d'you reckon on these two bits of hardboard nailed across a hole in the wood? Broken bits, at that."

"We could have done better with our stage scenery," agreed Scott with a snort, and promptly reached out to haul against the piece on top with his fingertips.

"No! No, don't do that, Scott!" squealed Rachel. "Somebody might come along and report us for breaking and entering, or something."

"Breaking and entering?" Scott laughed, pausing to suck a splinter from his finger. "Who'd want to break into this place, I'd like to know?"

"Looks like someone's had a go!" Jason called again. "Come and look over here, round the side of the building. Some of the wooden fencing's been trodden down, and just left."

The fencing had obviously been put up to protect one of the doors leading to Dreyton Manor. They could almost reach out and touch it through the spindly wooden palings and the rows of rusty wire which were meant to keep them all standing in a row.

The middle palings had given way first, and these now lay flat on the ground, with clumps of grass and thistles sprouting up between them. The rest lurched towards the doors on either side, the timbers black and slimy, and flecked with flakes of rust from the rotting hinges.

The only splash of colour came from a long split in the wood, through which tall spears of grass had pushed towards the light.

"Only needs one of us to get through," said Scott, already stepping across the palings to inspect the damage. The whole panel was warped and swollen with damp, little knots and splinters of wood spinning and whirling on cobwebby threads. It only needed one touch, he decided, for whole lumps of crumbly black timber to break away from the edges of the hole. He only hesitated because he was a good stage manager. "Never break anything up, unless you have to," he remembered Lynsey telling him, more than once. "Scenery and props are valuable, and you may easily need them again."

Besides, he thought, stroking the ornate hinges with some respect, it was still a door which someone had made with pride.

"Wait a sec!" he called at last. "If you can squeeze yourselves between the fencing and the edge of the door, there's a way in through this bit of wall that's caved in!"

They soon saw that the broken door was just about all that was left of the manor grounds. And that was only kept standing by half a collapsed archway, with a piece of the brick wall at either side. The rest was little more than a wilderness of rubble and stone, dotted here and there with clumps of dandelion and a few daisies. But there was hardly any rubbish to be seen. The hoarding which screened it from the view of the passers-by and cast such tall, dark shadows, also kept out most of the litter blown in from the motorway.

The only other landmark was an untidy circle of stones which had once been a rosebed. One last rose tree thrust its buds towards the sun, struggling to break free from the tangle of grass which they had glimpsed through the split in the door.

"It's a wonder the place is still standing," commented Rachel, turning her head towards the battered porch. "Beats me why anyone's bothered with chains and padlocks on the doors when most of the roof is missing!"

Tina did not answer. She was watching the boys hurrying on ahead, clambering over stumps of brick walls, and jumping across puddles where rainwater had filled deep ruts in the ground. She felt she quite understood why Rachel gave a deep sigh, before helping her across a short flight of stone steps, once leading into a room which now stood open and bare.

"Wonder if this could have been a kitchen or something?" she said, stepping carefully through a patch of rust-coloured tiles, cracked and misshapen with round humps of moss and thick weed.

"Mind you don't trip over just there!" Oliver yelled back helpfully.

"Yeah, that's right!" bellowed Jason. "I nearly caught my foot in an old bit of railing or something, with loads of grass growing over it!"

Not only broken railings, as Rachel and Tina soon discovered. Huge pieces of masonry bordered with plaster flowers and leaves, great slabs of black slate and red brick from the collapsed chimneys, all lay strewn around as they had fallen, half-hidden and forgotten.

"Not much further to go, Ratchet," Oliver shouted back again. "There's a bit just along here, by the side of the house, where the roof hasn't fallen in!"

By now the rain had made everywhere so slippery that Jason took pity on Rachel and Tina struggling along, and went back to give them a hand.

"Don't forget, you started all this!" he grinned, helping Rachel to wriggle through two bits of wall jutting out from the muddy ground. "Let's hope your *Merrie Devil of Dreyton* will be worth – "

"Now, what's up?" snapped Rachel, a streak of fair hair clinging damply to her forehead. "You know I can't stand people who don't finish what they're supposed to be saying!"

"Well ..." Jason began awkwardly, peering around through his rain-splattered spectacles. "This may sound ridiculous ..."

"What may sound ridiculous!"

"You mean — you mean, you didn't hear it?"

"Hear what?" Rachel screamed at him.

"Well ..." Jason paused and took a deep breath. "Just now, I-I'm sure I heard a horse whinnying."

Three

The three of them stood quite still, all listening hard. Jason kept turning his head this way and that, trying to work out the direction where the sound of the whinnying horse had come from. But, apart from the rain pattering down, all was quiet.

"Oh, this is crazy!" Rachel decided at last. "If there was a horse anywhere around here, surely we'd *see* it, not just hear it!"

Jason had to admit she was right. But Tina could see that he really believed he had heard something.

"Besides," Rachel went on, "the nearest stables are miles away, over at Broad Oak where we go for riding sessions at the academy. It must have been your dreamy imagination, Jason."

"Suppose so," sighed Jason, reluctantly following her across the last stretch of muddy ground to where Oliver was standing in the shelter of a half-ruined doorway.

There was an elaborate ironwork canopy overhead, thick with strands of ivy and bindweed creeping through the cracks in the walls.

Tina could hear nearly every raindrop trickling off the leaves and splashing softly on the grass and weeds at their feet. It seemed that hardly any sound reached them, not even from the motorway.

They moved on through the door but the boarded-up window frames soon made it too dark to see properly. In the end, they had to feel their way along the stone walls with their arms. Only a few thin shafts of daylight filtered through to light their way, and none of them liked the sour smell of damp and rotting timbers that seemed to linger everywhere.

The ground still felt moist and squelchy beneath their feet, although here and there they found themselves treading on tiles, which gave their steps an oddly lopsided echo.

"Sounds like a wooden leg tapping along," Jason remarked, trying to lighten the gloomy mood which they were all feeling.

This was enough to make Rachel grab Tina's wrist, looking back over her shoulder with a cry of terror.

"Jason! Do you you want to scare Tina out of her wits? You've already frightened her, going on about horses whinnying, when there aren't any."

"Only that one perched right at the top of the manor!" cut in Oliver unexpectedly. Tina was pleased that he had noticed. "Hey, Scotty! Where are you taking us?"

"Aw, stop moaning. Can't you see, there's a bit more light straight ahead? Could be part of a covered walkway, or entrance, or something. And I think there's a couple of benches against the wall, so we can have a break."

"Great!" The enthusiasm in Oliver's voice cheered them up and they stumbled forward with a new burst of energy.

"There's a bumpy bit just ahead, with iron loops or something in the ground!" Scott called back. "Best keep close to the wall . . . " His words faltered to a sudden stop, as a loud yell from Oliver resounded from one end of the passageway to the other. Jason stopped so suddenly that the two girls only just managed to save themselves from bumping into him.

"My — my head." Oliver was moaning, rubbing painfully. "Wh-what hit me?"

For an instant, everyone stood where they were,

listening. Only the rain plopping down between the bare rafters and broken roof slates broke the silence.

"Isn't that something fixed to the wall?" suggested Jason, gingerly stepping forward to get a closer look. "Could be a metal plate, or a plaque, or something." He began brushing away little clouds of dust, before scraping with his fingernails, then a piece of broken slate, until the letters stood out clearly enough for them all to read.

FELBOURNE URBAN DISTRICT COUNCIL
DREYTON MANOR
Open to the public from May to September
Wednesdays and Saturdays only 9:00am – 6:00pm
Visits can be arranged at other times by appointment with
the Curator, Felbourne Castle Museum.

"Felbourne Castle Museum," mused Oliver, quiet forgetting to rub his bruised head. "D'you reckon anyone there could tell us about *The Merrie Devil of Dreyton*?"

"Yeah! Worth a try, anyway," said Scott, determined to look on the bright side. "Anyone fancy a break?"

They sat down thankfully on the stone benches.

"Wonder where we are?" said Tina, screwing up her eyes to try and get a clearer look. "Just think – we might be sitting at the very spot where a squire sat, all those years ago."

"You're still thinking of yesterday's drama workshop," her brother interrupted.

"And if there was a squire," added Jason, "you can bet he'd be sitting somewhere a lot grander than this. Unless it was the stables, or the wine store, or something. Come on, Ollie, let's see if your map gives us any clues."

The map was carefully unfolded and spread across one of the benches. But it was too dark to pick out many of the details.

"This must have been where people came in, when Dreyton Manor was open," said Oliver, glancing ruefully in the direction of the metal plate. "I guess they must have come in through a side entrance, away from the doors at the front."

"Reckon you're right, Ollie." nodded Scott. "My dad says they called it the Tradesmen's Entrance in great big, old houses like this one."

He jumped to his feet. "Let's see where this passageway leads to, shall we? Or is it still raining? Funny how our voices echo in some parts and not in others, isn't it? Must be where the roof's given way in some places, eh?"

"Sssssh!" Oliver hissed at him. "Can't you shut up just for a minute?"

"Well!" Scott exploded. "I like that!"

Then he stopped, and an uneasy silence descended around them.

A silence broken only by the dull, uneven tap-tapping of footsteps coming towards them along the passageway.

Four

Nobody dared to move. The footsteps continued, becoming louder as they came closer. The passageway seemed darker and more sinister.

"Who – who is it?" whispered Tina, holding tight to Rachel. But the rest were too frightened to answer.

"Hel-lo!" came a voice, echoing towards them. "Any-one there?"

"D-don't scream!" Rachel hissed down at Tina. "Just keep quiet, and don't move!"

"Rachel?" came the voice again, sounding much more normal this time. "Rachel, is that you?"

"Lynsey!" cried Oliver with relief. "Lynsey, we – we thought – " He was glad when she broke into one of her infectious peals of laughter.

"I know what you thought, and it serves you right. Lucky for you I've got a good ear for stage whispers, Oliver Davis. Do you know you're not supposed to be here?"

"But there's no 'Keep Out' notice or anything," Jason objected, quick to come to Oliver's defence.

"Just because there are a few holes in the fencing doesn't give everyone right of way! Trip over one of those gigantic pieces of masonry outside, and you could easily break a leg or something. Why are you rubbing your head, Oliver?"

"Hurt myself," he admitted, and hoped she wouldn't see that he was going red. "On that metal plate over there."

"It says that Dreyton Manor was run by the Felbourne Castle Museum," announced Rachel, eager to change the subject. "D'you think they'll know anything about the Merrie Devil, Lynsey?"

"Shouldn't be at all surprised," Lynsey smiled, slipping a bulging holdall from her shoulder so that it thudded down on one of the benches. "And I know someone else who could tell you quite a bit, as well."

"Who?" they all cried together.

"Peter Albany-Smith. Told you I'd be seeing him last night, didn't I? But before I tell you about that, let's have some coffee," and she put an end to any more questions with a wave of her hand. "And let me tell you, you're lucky to have all this. It was only because Rachel's mother mentioned Dreyton Manor when I telephoned that I guessed where you'd gone."

"We all thought you were a a ghost, or something, Lynsey," Rachel giggled, quite forgetting how scared she had been. "Jason started us off, saying he heard a horse whinnying."

"A horse whinnying?" Lynsey seemed quite calm as she began taking an assortment of cups and beakers from her holdall and setting them out on the bench. "Well, that's understandable when you think of that lovely stone horse high up, outside."

She turned her head, and Rachel could see her thoughtful expression.

"I just wonder if it's anything to do with the Merrie Devil." She glanced around at their puzzled faces and laughed again. "It's only because Peter says that the Merrie Devil was most probably a blacksmith! Not a real devil with horns and a tail after all, you see!"

"A blacksmith?" Oliver repeated, brown eyes widening in amazement. "But why would a blacksmith be called the Merrie Devil?"

"You're forgetting that everyone depended on horses once upon a time. Farming, travelling, work. Nobody could get far without them. So, because blacksmiths had such

26

power, they were always treated with great respect just in case they had any magic to use against people they didn't like."

"Peter Albany-Smith told you all that?" Jason could hardly believe his ears.

"Told you, he's not really the doddering old fool most people think! Apparently, blacksmiths crop up in all sorts of old legends and pantomimes!"

"But, who *was* the Merrie Devil of Dreyton?" persisted Oliver. "Apart from being a blacksmith, I mean! What was his name?"

"I work in a tax office, not a detective agency!" Lynsey reminded him cheerfully. "Now, who wants some coffee? Then you can show me this plaque, or whatever it is."

They moved to the end of the passageway where the light was better and had a look at Oliver's map and the photographs.

"Must have been a beautiful place in the old days," Lynsey said at last, as she handed Tina's photographs back.

"And did you see that every path on the map leads towards the manor?" added Oliver eagerly. "I bet it was the most important place for miles around, the place where everyone came."

"Including the Merrie Devil," put in Rachel, which was exactly what they were all thinking. "How about seeing what we can find at Felbourne Castle Museum, Lynsey? It's only a couple of stops on the train."

"Well," Lynsey hesitated. "Maybe we could all go there next Saturday seeing as our workshop's been cancelled. I had a telephone message this morning. That's why I wanted to see you."

"Someone else booked the Parish Hall, then?" snapped Oliver. "Why should we always be the ones who get kicked out?"

"Because it's the only way we could get the Parish Hall, Oliver. When I started up the Studio Workshop three years ago, nobody knew how popular it was going to be. So we were only meant to be staying at the Parish Hall until we found somewhere else we could afford! Still," she brightened up, "at least we can go to Felbourne Castle Museum next Saturday, eh? There's a nice little costume gallery there, with farming tools on show, and an old-fashioned kitchen."

"Sounds like it's worth the trip!" said Scott. "Even without the Merrie Devil of Dreyton!"

They grinned around at each other, Oliver beginning to rub his hands together, as he always did when he was pleased about something.

"And we wouldn't have known anything about Dreyton Manor being run by the Museum if we hadn't made up our minds to come here and see what we could find!" Jason pointed out, Rachel looking at him with clear admiration. "Right, Lynsey?"

"OK, Jason," she chuckled. "I get the message. Look, let's get out in the open, shall we? The rain's stopped, thank goodness, so the air should be a bit fresher than it is in here."

Very slowly, they felt their way along to the end of the passage, and out into a small courtyard, at the back of the manor house.

"Well! It doesn't look half so bad from this side" said Scott, and none of the others argued.

The front of the manor had seemed so dark and brooding. There was nothing to shine or to wink in the sun, no life in the dull plywood, no colour in the cracked tiles and broken slates. Nothing moved or made a sound.

But although the back was even more seriously damaged in some places, one or two tiny windows still remained in odd corners of the building, catching the light as the clouds raced overhead.

The wind rustled through the grass and the weeds growing in spaces in the brickwork. There was the gurgle of rainwater running along gutters and down drainpipes, with noisy sparrows splashing and drinking and squabbling in little puddles.

"Wish we could get right inside, somehow!" Oliver said at last, clanking the massive padlocks and chains which fastened the huge wooden doors set into the wall. "See that porch or balcony or whatever it is up there looks a bit like a bird cage, over the top of those big French windows? Well, there's a door behind that, and I'm pretty sure it's not shut properly."

"Where?" asked Rachel, Tina craning her neck, as well. "Where?"

"You could be right, Oliver," Lynsey butted in. "But perhaps it's because more birds are nesting up there, and all the straw and stuff has wedged the door open!"

As if to confirm her words there was a chorus of squawking and a whole cloud of jackdaws flew out all at once, wings flapping like black fans.

"Wonder what scared them?" said Jason, watching the birds wheeling and circling around. "D'you think they've just realized we're here?"

"Probably," Oliver agreed. "It's been ages since this place had any visitors, that's for sure."

"Wish we knew what it's like inside!" added Tina. Then Scott squinted through the gap where   mework of one of the doors had warped away fr
surround, trying to see what was there

"Looks like part of a great big garde
a few minutes. "You know, where ric
and dances and all that." He squinte

"And there's a long sort of stone patio, with steps leading down onto the grass. Make a smashing stage, that would."

"Sounds lovely!" cried Lynsey, and almost pushed Scott out of the way so that she could put her eye to the crack, too. "Oh, if only we could find out a bit more about this *Merrie Devil of Dreyton*. Then the Council might even let us come here when the Parish Hall's being used, at least until the anniversary celebrations."

The others all crowded round the crack, wanting to peer through. Only Tina stayed near the fountain, scuffing among the dusty remains with the toe of her shoe then tugging at a few wet clumps of greenery which had grown through the cracks in the stone.

"Tina!" Scott wailed in exasperation. "Just what d'you think you're doing?"

"Counting up how many horseshoes I can find carved round the edges," she replied. "Bit funny for a water fountain, isn't it?"

Oliver was the first to dash across the courtyard, Lynsey noted with amusement, and watched as he began to pull handfuls of weed and creeper away from the stone, making whole colonies of woodlice and beetles scurry for shelter.

"Might be a badge, or a crest, or something," he suggested. "Look, they're all around the sides of the fountain, and the trough, as well."

"And that all fits in with Tina's golden horse," Scott burst out. "You know, I just bet this place has got something to do with *The Merrie Devil of Dreyton*, don't you, Ollie? What d'you reckon, Jason?"

But Jason was not there. Almost without knowing it, he had backed away out of the courtyard and into a deserted stretch of grass, flanked by a line of stone arches.

From the skeletons of the smaller columns and huge star ¬s set within each of the arches, it was clear that this had once been a line of stained glass windows looking out on to another part of the estate.

But Jason only gave them a brief glance before lifting his gaze towards the sky, and the blazing golden hooves of the horse at the top of the manor.

Whilst all the time, the sound of a horse whinnying drifted clearly towards him.

And this time he was sure someone else could hear the horse, too. Because she was crying. Crying as if her heart would break.

Five

Just for a moment, Jason felt as if the sounds were all around him, half expecting the others to start shouting that they could hear a horse and a girl crying, too.

Then, with the next hiss of wind through the trees, he was telling himself again that the whole thing was ridiculous.

Here he was, he argued fiercely, standing in the ruins of an old estate which had been empty for years, as the weeds, the rubble, the blocked-up water fountain and everything else clearly proved. So what sort of horse was it that he could hear, yet could not see? A horse, he reasoned, was a big animal. Where could it get in? The five of them had found it difficult enough. Where could it be kept?

"Ah, here's Jason," came Lynsey's clear voice. "Been trying to find another way out, have you?"

"Er, sort of . . ." he faltered, glad when Oliver interrupted with his usual enthusiasm.

"Doesn't seem to be any other gaps or broken bits in the hoarding or anywhere else, does there? We'll just have to walk through that passageway again, and out along the side of the house."

The passageway was every bit as dark and smelly as they remembered, the ground seeming even wetter and muddier than when they had first squeezed through the wooden palings and stepped across the broken wall.

The others chattered eagerly, about the manor house, the discovery of the plaque from Felbourne Castle

Museum, and the wonderful natural stage and auditorium they'd found at the back of the building.

But, for Jason, it all passed like some peculiar, misty sort of dream, strange and unreal.

Only when Rachel had waved a cheery goodbye, and he was on his own again, had he made up his mind for sure.

All this talk of horses and Dreyton's Merrie Devil turning out to be a blacksmith had probably put ideas into his head. Could happen to anyone. Horses whinnying and girls sobbing ... well, it all had to do with something else, something he'd get to know about before long.

But just to talk things through he decided to call round at Oliver's next day. He needed to borrow a T-shirt for school on Wednesday, he reminded himself.

"What's so special about one T-shirt?" persisted Mark, his elder brother, busily packing his telephone engineer's toolbag. "I've got loads I can lend you!"

"I – I need one in the school colours! We're having trials for the cricket team!"

"Cricket?" Mark exploded, laughing loudly enough for their mum and dad, working in the gift shop below their maisonette, to wonder what the joke was. "Since when have you been interested in cricket? You've never even—"

But Jason was already hurrying down the stairs and out the back way.

It was only a ten minute walk to Oliver's house near the Civic Centre, but he opted for the long way round, through Halstead Park.

He needed time to think, he told himself for the hundredth time, staring blankly across the duck pond.

Dreyton Manor was a huge place, as Oliver's map had shown. It would take anyone ages to get around and see every single bit that was left standing. The sounds could have come from anywhere.

Or could he have heard only crying, and thought there was a horse whinnying as well?

"Watch out lad!" shouted the park keeper, waving a hand at him. "Do you want to be run down by the grass-cutter?"

Jason hastily retraced his steps back to the main path. Perhaps, he comforted himself, Oliver would know some of the answers. He usually did.

It took Oliver a bit longer than usual to come to the door, but he seemed pleased to see Jason.

"Just in time to give me a hand with that maths project we were set," he announced. "I've been trying to puzzle it out for hours."

"I know just how that feels," Jason answered with a sigh. Then he saw all the leaflets spread over Oliver's bed, and gave a smile instead. "Your maths project seems a bit different to mine, though."

"Well, we didn't have much chance to go through this lot, did we? Not that it tells us much, only about the royal charter being given to the town, how Dreyton has grown over the years, all that sort of stuff. Nothing about blacksmiths, or horses, or — "

"What made you say that, Ollie?" Jason broke in. "About horses, I mean?" Oliver looked quite surprised.

"Blacksmiths usually look after horses, don't they? Why do you ask?"

"Oh, I don't know," Jason fibbed, turning away, just slightly. "Only wondered, that's all. Oliver — "

"Ummmm?" Oliver was too intent on tidying the bed to notice Jason's twitching fingers, or the way he kept biting his bottom lip.

"You — you don't believe in — in ghosts, do you?"

"I — I don't think I do, not really. But if you'd asked me that at Dreyton Manor, with the wind howling around and

34

everywhere so quiet ... Hearing Lynsey's footsteps tapping along put the shakes up all of us, didn't it?".

"Sure did!" agreed Jason with a reminiscent chuckle.

It hadn't exactly been the sort of answer he'd wanted to hear but Oliver was already pulling down the desk-flap of the bureau his dad had made for him, revealing an untidy heap of papers with a calculator and ruler on top.

At least, Jason thought with another sigh, he knew where he was when it came to facts and figures.

Someone else was interested in facts and figures, too, and that was Rachel, scribbling furiously in the middle of an English lesson at St Helena's Academy:

Anniversary celebrations – July 18th/19th
Dress rehearsal – 12th July. Costumes finished by 7th.
Scenery ready – 1st July.
Cast to be word perfect by end of June, latest.

And the last four words were underlined, more than once.

"That's only three months to get the script together," Rachel muttered to herself, "then get all the parts sorted out, props ready – "

"Costumes to be made, of course," a smooth voice cut in. "Not to mention the scenery."

"Right!" cried Rachel, blissfully unaware of all the giggling that was going on but almost leaping into the air when a large hand slammed down on her desk.

"Rachel," cooed Miss Watson with a sickly-sweet smile. "Rachel, dear, do you think you could possibly attend to this exercise in English grammar?"

"Sorry, Miss Watson." It wasn't often that Rachel felt flustered about anything. "Only, I – I was thinking of this

35

play. For the Dreyton Anniversary, you know!" She dearly wanted to explain but Miss Watson was not the sort of teacher to be side-tracked from her lessons. "It — it's about this blacksmith — "

"Yes, dear, I quite understand. The whole class is upset at having to do extra English, instead of riding lessons at Broad Oak."

"Why couldn't we go to Broad Oak?" enquired Jessica, the girl at the next desk.

"I don't really know. Apparently, there's been some sort of virus infection, and one or two of the horses are out of action for the time being." There was a chorus of moans and groans. "Yes, I know it's disappointing!" she went on. "Not least because Rachel Oldham might have met a blacksmith who could tell her exactly how to stage this wonderful play of hers."

The moans and groans changed to a ripple of amusement, and Rachel was annoyed to find herself blushing. But deep inside, her heart began pounding with excitement, and she scribbled another item on her list:

Broad Oak Stables. Put workshop in touch with blacksmith to help with costumes and props?

Once again, she caught Miss Watson's disapproving eye, and hastily stuffed the notebook underneath her pencil case.

If only she could talk things over with somebody at break, she thought longingly. As it was, half the girls in her class were boarders at the academy, going home at weekends, and she was the only one who travelled from Dreyton each day, driven to school by her father, who was also the academy's accountant.

After school, it was usually Mrs Oldham who came to

drive Rachel home — though not usually with such an impatient tooting of the horn by the main gate.

"Sorry to hurry you along darling," her mother apologized, "but we must get home early. The Stagecoach Group are coming round this evening, you see. We're thinking of doing a musical revue for the 600 Years of Dreyton celebrations."

"That's all I seem to be hearing about," Rachel muttered.

"Yes, I know, dear." Her mother gave a merry little laugh. "Isn't it exciting?"

"Hairy, I'd call it. Mummy, you know the Studio Workshop's started on this *Merrie Devil of Dreyton* idea, don't you? Well, I worked out the timetable this afternoon and if we don't soon get some sort of script, we're in real trouble. There's the trip to Felbourne Castle Museum on Saturday, but — "

"That used to be the county headquarters. The records library is still there, I believe."

"Records library?" Rachel repeated with interest. "So, will they help us to track down this *Merrie Devil of Dreyton* play?"

"Why not telephone and ask?" Mrs Oldham suggested. "It's only just four o'clock now, and I wouldn't have thought they'd close for at least another hour."

Then came the second impatient blast on the horn that afternoon. "Out of the way, you stupid girl. Fancy stopping halfway across a pedestrian crossing with her mouth open. I ask you."

"That's Tina, Scotty's sister from drama workshop!" yelled Rachel, frantically winding the window down. "Hey, Tina! Mummy says what about phoning Felbourne right now, to ask about the script for the *Merrie Devil of Dreyton*?"

"But what if they say they can't help?" Tina shouted back. "Does that mean the Saturday trip is called off?"

"I — I didn't think about that," Rachel admitted, thrown off her guard by the line of cars queuing up behind and sounding quite a fanfare on their horns.

"Oh, get her inside for heaven's sake, Rachel!" Mrs Oldham cried. "We're holding up all the traffic."

"Look, let's sort it out at home," Rachel gabbled on, leaning awkwardly across the back of her seat to open a rear door. "You can phone Scotty to say you'll be a bit late, can't you? We can have some sandwiches or something before Mummy's friends from Stagecoach come round, then she can run you home. That's all right, isn't it, Mummy?"

Tina could see Mrs Oldham smiling into the car mirror and grinned back at her.

When they got home Tina phoned Scott to say she'd be late and then Rachel dialled the museum.

"Er — script for *Merrie Devil of Dreyton*?" repeated the female voice at the other end, hesitating just a little. "Yes, Yes, I think we may be able to help you — "

"Terrific!" Rachel broke in, giving a triumphant thumbs up sign to Tina across the hall.

"I — er — I shall have to ring you back, of course," Rachel was much too excited to hear that the woman sounded rather unsure of herself. "But I think it should be before the end of the afternoon."

Sure enough, the telephone rang not long afterwards.

"That's for us, Mummy," Rachel called out in the direction of the kitchen. "Hello? Dreyton Heath 451 ... Yes, I was the one who asked about — What? You've actually got the script?"

Her voice rose to such a high-pitched squeal that Tina darted towards her, straining to hear all that was being said.

"It's a very old manuscript," Rachel was informed, "sent

38

to the Lord Chamberlain in 1839 so that a licence could be granted for public performance in London."

"So, can we borrow it?" Rachel persisted.

"You can make a copy," came the reply, "but that would have to be done here. The original manuscript is the only one we have, you see, so we could not possibly risk damage by allowing it to be removed from our files for photocopying or anything of that sort."

"Tell her we'll get it copied at the museum on Saturday, then," Tina hissed over Rachel's shoulder. "We'll take it in turns, each writing out a page."

"Ahem," interrupted the voice. "There is just one other thing."

"Yes?" Rachel flapped a hand at Tina to keep her quiet.

"I — er — I think I should tell you that someone else has been enquiring about *The Merrie Devil of Dreyton*. The manuscript has already been reserved for their use."

Six

Tina wished she could do something. She felt awkward just standing there, watching Rachel swallowing hard and gripping the telephone with both hands.

"You couldn't tell me who else wants to see the *Merrie Devil of Dreyton* script, could you?" she asked. "Our workshop is thinking of putting on the same production, and — "

"Oh, but the young lady is French," the librarian interrupted, loud enough for Tina to overhear. "At least, I've written her name down as Marie Du Ville, a student from a boarding school in Paris."

Rachel was too stunned to answer.

"Must say, I was surprised to get two requests for the same manuscript in one afternoon," the woman went on. "Most extraordinary."

"Yes ..." Rachel raised a hand to her forehead, trying to think clearly. "So, what about us, then?"

"Well, as long as you don't both arrive on the same day, there's nothing to stop you making your own copy. May I have your name?"

Dumbly, Tina listened as Rachel gave all the details, the same questions racing through both their minds.

Why was *The Merrie Devil of Dreyton* so important to this Marie Du Ville, whoever she was? How had she found the play, when Lynsey had said that even the organizers of the Dreyton Anniversary had never heard of it? If she came from a school in Paris, where was she staying?

"Could take ages trying to find all that out," was Scott's verdict, when Tina asked his advice. "After all, why shouldn't she be a French student, like the library woman said?"

"But, what about her phoning up for the same script, on exactly the same day as us?"

"How many times have you wanted to borrow something of mine that I'd just lent to someone else?" Scott retorted, with a maddening shrug of his shoulders. "Or I've needed something that Mum's thrown away the day before? You and Rachel have more or less got the script, haven't you?"

"Yes, but — "

"But, nothing. Jason and Oliver won't worry about Marie what's-her-name turning up out of nowhere when Rachel tells them, you'll see."

He only wished he could have sounded a bit more convincing. Never mind, he comforted himself, not long to go before they would be on their way to the Castle Museum. Then they could look forward to getting their teeth into a script, and getting on with the production.

As the Saturday morning train sped towards Felbourne they went over their plans.

"Now," Oliver said, "we've agreed that it'll be Jason and me doing the copying, OK? And Rachel's coming in with us."

"What about me and Tina?" demanded Scott, who always hated being left out of things.

"You'll be scouring around for any more clues about the blacksmith, or Dreyton Manor. I still think the place is tied up somewhere in all this."

Tina shivered a little.

"You make it all sound so — so sort of strange, Oliver," she said. "As if someone's behind us all the time, watching everything we do ..."

41

"Baby," scoffed Scott, yet with an uncomfortable feeling that they all knew exactly what his sister meant.

"Felbourne, next stop!" Lynsey announced suddenly, leading the way to the carriage doors. "Everyone ready? Don't leave anything behind."

Oliver and Jason remembered visiting Castle Museum with their school. It was a low, red brick building, surrounded on three sides by a wall with narrow little window slots and a line of bricks set into the top, trying to look like a real castle.

It was this which had given the place its name, along with a fine arched gateway and cobbled path leading up to the main entrance.

"Everyone except Oliver, Jason and Rachel into the main exhibition room, then on to the costume gallery," commanded Lynsey. "Think about the history of Dreyton we were working on last Saturday, and see what notes and sketches you can make of the props and outfits you'll need."

There were quite a few smiles and enthusiastic grins at this but Tina and Scott were watching Rachel and Jason, following Oliver towards a door with the sign "Reference Library. Please knock and enter."

"Studio Workshop?" smiled the grey-haired lady at the desk, and took a pencil from the pocket of her blue overall. "Rachel Oldham reserved the *Merrie Devil of Dreyton* script for you, didn't she?"

"Yes, that's me," Rachel introduced herself, and the librarian lifted up the desk flap so that they could pass through into a smaller room.

"Wait here, and I'll bring the manuscript with pencils and paper."

"Need any help?" Rachel enquired politely.

"No, it — it's all right," the librarian puffed, bearing a huge, thick book towards the only available table, where

42

the two boys sat waiting. "I think the script is the first in this volume. The bookmark's in the right place anyway, from the other young lady."

So the mysterious Marie Du Ville has already been and gone, thought Rachel, but said nothing.

The two boys were already turning the grey pages. "*The Merrie Devil of Dreyton!*" Oliver read aloud. "*The Merrie Devil of Dreyton — or, The Whispering Chamber.* Hey! That sounds good, doesn't it?"

Rather gingerly, he began tracing the faded lines of writing with his forefinger, Jason and Rachel standing close together and reading over his shoulder, translating the old-fashioned 'f' style letter 's' with some difficulty.

*THE MERRIE DEVIL OF DREYTON
(or THE WHISPERING CHAMBER)
Main Characters
JOHN GABRIEL blacksmith, The Merrie Devil of Dreyton
FIREFLY his magical spirit
MASTER RICHARD GILES a rich miller
MATHILDA miller's only daughter
EDWIN Mathilda's sweetheart
LORD CUTHBERT suitor to Mathilda
SQUIRE MELROSE Squire of Dreyton*

"John Gabriel," breathed Rachel. "Now we know his name."

"Plenty of good parts," Jason added, leaning over and trying to turn the next page. "Looks like a good plot, too."

"About two men wanting to marry the same girl," Rachel chimed in, getting quite carried away. "One's the good guy — that'll be Edwin — and I bet Lord Cuthbert's the baddy. We'll need somebody tall and dark like you for that, Jason, and — "

43

"Look, shut up, both of you!" Oliver very nearly flung down his pencil. "Fat chance we've got of copying this thing with you nattering away!"

"You've got a cheek, Oliver!" Rachel burst out. "When I was the one who — "

But Oliver was prepared for one of her outbursts.

"If you want to make yourself really useful, go and find out what Tina and Scotty are doing! Otherwise, we'll never get this done."

"Come on, Ratchet," said Jason, grabbing her hand and making for the door. "Better leave him in peace."

Once outside, Rachel took a deep breath and gave a happy sigh. "Wonder if they've got any costume ideas for Mathilda?" she said.

There was quite a crowd in the costume gallery, but Rachel picked out Tina's flaming red hair in front of one of the largest displays on show — a plaster-cast anvil set against the crude wooden door of a forge. Scott was crouching in front of it, sketching busily on a scrap of paper.

But what interested Rachel was the figure beside the anvil — somebody fairly tall and broad-shouldered, wearing high boots and a leather apron, with a jerkin which laced up the front.

"What do you think?" Tina asked quietly. "Bit of a surprise, isn't it, after we've been talking about black-smiths?"

"You can say that again," Rachel agreed. "This Merrie Devil must be important, somehow! And it's all to do with something we don't know about! Not yet, anyway . . ."

Jason left Rachel to tell Scott and Tina about John Gabriel, the characters in the play, the basic plot, and everything else.

Might as well go back to the library, he decided, his

shoes squeaking on the polished floor. Wait till Ollie heard there was a complete blacksmith's outfit and part of an actual set in the little costume gallery. Like Rachel said, it must mean something.

"Glad you're back," Oliver greeted him, seeming in a much better mood, although he was rubbing his right hand and wrist and wincing a little. "I'm about halfway through."

"No kidding? I thought it'd take ages."

"Well, it hasn't all been written out, only enough to give the general idea. See?"

"Lord Cuthbert goes to kiss Mathilda's hand," Jason read, "but she turns away. Cuthbert hurries off to greet Squire Melrose, and Edwin enters in shabby dress. Mathilda greets him warmly."

"Seems that Edwin is John Gabriel's friend," Oliver butted in, giving his wrist another rub.

"The Squire enters," Jason continued. "The miller introduces Lord Cuthbert and his daughter!"

> *Your daughter, sir? Then if she likes to be*
> *A lady's maid, she can come with me!*
> *Along with her sweetheart, she will live right well.*
> *A good master, I, as all my friends can tell.*

"Mathilda turns away from Cuthbert," Jason continued to read, "and gives her hand to Edwin. Good bit of writing to do, but that doesn't matter, does it?"

He sat down and began writing. Oliver stood reading over his shoulder and took the part of the squire.

> *We'll settle this! Now, all round, attend!*
> *To Dreyton, now, both sweethearts we will send!*
> *And he who dares to sleep all night*
> *In my Whispering Chamber, without fear or fright*

45

Shall win the girl! Good Cuthbert, don't be taunted!
For, by my ruff, I can't believe 'tis haunted!"

"Ummm," muttered Jason, head bent over the desk. "Can't say I think much of the rhyme."

"Never mind the rhyme," said Oliver slowly. "What about the words? And this haunted Whispering Chamber?"

"Ummmm ..." said Jason again. "Where Cuthbert and Edwin have got to spend the night ... Looks like Scotty gets his spooks, after all."

"But, don't you see?" Oliver persisted. "It's *Squire Melrose*, the name on those postcards you and Tina bought, right?"

"Right!" Jason put down his pencil, beginning to see the connection.

"And Squire Melrose talks about spending the night in *my* Whispering Chamber. The Whispering Chamber belonged to him."

"So, the Whispering Chamber," finished Jason, "the Whispering Chamber must be — "

"Yes!" Oliver cut in. "It must be at Dreyton Manor!"

Seven

Jason guessed what Oliver was going to say next.

"We've got to go back to Dreyton Manor. I knew all along that place was mixed up with the Merrie Devil."

"Keep your voice down," Jason hissed, looking around for the lady librarian. "And don't forget, Lynsey's got to know about the Whispering Chamber when she types out the script."

"What does that matter? For all she knows, it's only part of an old story."

"Yes, but ..." Jason hesitated, wondering what the mysterious Marie Du Ville had made of it all. Had she puzzled over the whereabouts of the Whispering Chamber? Or thought nothing of it?

"Look," Oliver was saying, and Jason could hear he was trying to be patient. "Look, let's get the copying done – we might learn a bit more while we're doing it."

And so they scribbled on, sitting side by side at the table with the book open between them, each copying out a page at a time.

For Jason it was a long, painstaking task, with a good deal of sighing and pencil-chewing. But Oliver's broad fingers moved more quickly along the lines of script, his brown eyes darting back and forth as he wrote.

It took another hour of solid writing before the copying was finally completed. But seeing how pleased and excited the others were at actually getting the long-lost script made Oliver and Jason decide that it had all been worthwhile.

"Perfect," declared Rachel, which just about summed up

everyone's feelings about *The Merrie Devil*. "Just think what we could do with this Whispering Chamber!"

"I've just thought," said Rachel, fishing in her jacket pocket, "the academy gave us all a note yesterday about riding lessons at Broad Oak next week. I was going to ask about borrowing some of their props." She pulled out a crumpled strip of paper, and gave another snort. "That's no good. It's only the bookmark from the reading library."

"Let's see that a sec, Ratchet," said Jason, reading then re-reading the name: "Marie Du Ville ... Marie Du Ville ..." until Oliver could stand it no longer.

"Give it a rest, Jason! OK, so she's read the script, but we've got it now, haven't we? And she's French, anyway."

"French," Jason muttered to himself, wondering why he felt so uneasy.

Tina noticed that he kept studying the bookmark all the way home in the train.

It was only at the end of the journey, just as Dreyton Lock station came in sight, that the puzzle became clearer. Jason opened his mouth to call across to Oliver, then shut it again. Best to make absolutely sure, he decided. No sense in spoiling all the fun and excitement of watching his dad's photocopier churning out page after page of the script, with everyone eager to start reading their favourite parts.

His dad had said they could use his photocopier to copy the script. When they were halfway through, Lynsey called to see how they were getting on.

"So many good characters!" she exclaimed. "Country people, men working in the mill and the dairymaids. It all fits in with what we've done already."

She began stacking the finished pages in neat piles, ready for Tina to staple together.

"First thing on Monday, I'm entering this for the Dreyton

48

Anniversary Celebrations. We'll never get anything better than this, I'm sure."

"Great!" breathed Rachel, beaming across at Tina.

"Terrific!" agreed Oliver.

"Like to give me and Shirley a hand typing it out tomorrow, Jason?" Shirley was Lynsey's next-door neighbour, as well as being Studio Workshop's wardrobe mistress, coffee lady, and lots more besides. "You can type a bit, can't you?" Lynsey went on. "Anyway, give me a call if you can manage it. And I'll meet you at *Marigold's* on the way home from work on Wednesday to fix up the first read-through, right?"

This brought another round of smiles and excited glances from everybody.

Everybody, that is, except Jason. Tina noticed he was a bit withdrawn. "Going to be a nice day tomorrow," she forecast, looking up at the pink sky. "Dreyton Manor will seem a different place with the sun shining."

"Yes." His green eyes seemed so troubled.

"Jason, you're not still thinking about about that horse whinnying and the person crying and everything, are you? Because, if you are — "

"No!" Jason answered, and Tina had to believe him.

The strange thing was that Jason didn't turn up at the clock tower when they all met up to go to Dreyton Manor the following afternoon.

"Probably helping Lynsey, after all," said Oliver, after they'd waited for what seemed like ages. "Might have told us, though."

"Might be coming on later," suggested Scott. "He knows where we are, anyway!" And with that he led the way to the manor.

They soon found the gap alongside the broken fencing,

49

squeezing their way through into the grounds and then along the covered passageway.

"We'll find another way in for next time," Oliver promised. "We're coming up to the Felbourne Museum sign, so it can't be much further."

Scott was already well ahead, the familiar mop of red hair disappearing around a corner of the ruined courtyard almost before the rest of them had struggled across the last patch of broken tiles and out into the daylight.

"Hurry up!" he shouted. "Can't you go any quicker?"

"Give us a chance, Scotty," Oliver yelled back at him, annoyed that he was so far ahead.

Scott was debating whether it would be simpler just to climb over the wall to get into the manor, when a flutter of cabbage white butterflies made him stop close to a ragged line of overgrown brambles. Another part of the gardens, he supposed idly, beginning to tug and pull at the straggly branches, very nearly falling over as the whole line lurched towards the ground.

When he tried straightening up, his knuckles grazed against something cold and hard. Sharply, he drew back his hand, freckled face creasing into a broad grin as he brushed away a shower of tawny rust.

"Over here!" he shouted. "There's some railings or a gate or something, pushed down by the weight of these bushes. I can see right through to that open air stage."

It was easy after that. A matter of a few more armfuls of brambles to be twisted off or broken away, then squeezing through the rest and they were right inside, standing so close to the manor house that Tina had to crane her neck to look up at the birdcage balcony with the half-open window beyond.

Scott had gone ahead again. "Down here!" he shouted.

"See? Along by the bottom of the steps. Open your eyes, Ollie!"

Through the gloom they could just make out an arched doorway, with stone steps rising up beyond it towards a tiny, square window, almost completely grown over by ivy which flapped in the breeze.

"Wine cellars?" wondered Oliver.

"Coal, probably," Scott whispered back. "See that circle of light in the roof? Bet that's a coal hole cover, like the one in front of the Parish Hall."

At the top, they both paused to get their breath back, then Scott struggled to pull up the stiff iron latch and push the window open, creaking and groaning in protest.

Scott poked his head out first, and gave a long, low whistle. "I don't believe it! I — I just don't believe it!"

"What?" demanded Oliver, trying to squeeze in beside Scott.

"Hoof prints. See, near that old-fashioned water pump, where the ground's still a bit muddy? And there was us thinking old Jason was round the twist, rambling on about hearing horses."

"Probably a gypsy, or a rider who got a bit lost," Oliver suggested, his voice rising with excitement. "They must have seen those old horseshoes in the wall over there, and thought it was a riding school, or stables or something."

"That's where the blacksmith worked," said Scott, his keen eyes picking out all the details of a long, flat building with its slate roof. "Or at least the place where he came to shoe the horses. We must be able to get a closer look."

They left the window and peered through the gloom, looking for another way out. They seemed to be in some sort of hall, judging by the wisps of sunlight stretching out like skinny fingers from underneath two or three huge doors. There was something rustling somewhere behind them, and

51

something else banging softly up ahead. But there was something else too — like somebody crying out, a voice rising to a wail then dying away into a strangled-sounding sob. Scott strained to hear it, but heard instead the unmistakable sound of a key grating in a rusty lock, and a door grinding open nearby.

It was then Scott knew exactly how it felt to be rooted to the spot, as if both legs were made of lead, too heavy and too cold to run, or even move.

Something had disturbed the dust which lay all about them, and it whirled up into a fine misty curtain. A curtain through which they could pick out a tall, black shadow with high boots, stamping out into the hall.

Eight

For one dreadful moment, Scott thought he was going to scream, but his mouth just gaped wide open. His throat felt so tight and so dry that no sound came.

Next minute, the door slammed shut, echoing through the hall. Rachel and Tina heard it outside.

"Probably Scott and Ollie finding their way around," Rachel guessed. "Must say, they've been gone long enough! Now, if we can finish working out where to mark centre stage — " and she went back to her calculations. Tina was still listening for the noise. "There it is, again!" she butted in. She rushed over and peered through the gigantic French windows, trying to see inside. "See these shutters on the other side? Look, someone's trying to pull them back. Scott! Oliver! We're out here! Can't you get the windows open?"

There was no answer, except for the rumble of old wood and the creaking of hinges.

Slowly, a thin crack began appearing, becoming wider and wider until an arm and a hand managed to squeeze through the shutters, groping around for the rusty bolt.

"It's opening!" squealed Tina, reaching for the window again. "It's opening!"

"Do you think I don't know that?" the answer came back in a muffled growl. "You've got to pull on your side, not push."

It needed a lot more pushing and pulling to get the window open, and then only wide enough for a very muddy pair of green wellingtons to shuffle out into the daylight.

"Jason!" gasped Rachel. "Where did you spring from?"

"There's someone inside," Jason spluttered, "two I think."

53

"That's Oliver and Scott," said Rachel, matter of factly.

"But I thought — " started Jason, but he was interrupted by another voice from inside the building.

"Hey! Somebody come and help me and Ollie through this window! We've got to get out of here, fast!"

Jason, Tina and Rachel raced towards the voice.

"Through this bit of hedge!" Jason commanded. "There's some stables on the other side, near to a rusty old water pump!"

Jason's directions proved correct, but Scott had wriggled free by the time they reached him.

"Back inside, Ollie!" Jason ordered through the half-open window, ignoring Oliver's shouts of indignation. "Go along the hall and through the first door you come to. We've got the windows open, so there's some more light coming through."

"How do you know the way out?" faltered Scott, pointing an accusing finger. "You you weren't the one who came into the hall just now, stamping and slamming doors? Why didn't you give a shout, or something?"

"I didn't realize you were in there. All I knew was that I'd found another way in through the courtyard!" Jason retorted. "I thought I was in the Whispering Chamber!"

"The Whispering Chamber?" echoed Rachel in delight. "Is it really the room leading out onto our stage?"

"Let's go and have a look," Jason offered, helping her to squeeze back through the hedge. "Ollie must be nearly there by now."

Oliver could only hear snatches of this conversation, and he couldn't quite decide whether to feel annoyed with himself for being so frightened by Jason, or glad that he'd at last found a way out into the sunshine.

When they were all together again they folded back the shutters where Jason had appeared so they could see into the huge room with its blackened walls and high ceilings.

"Doesn't look like a Whispering Chamber," Scott said flatly. "Our voices sound funny, but that's only because the place is empty."

"Be all right for rehearsals, though," Oliver pointed out. "Much better than anything we could rig up in the Parish Hall."

"Lynsey said it would be marvellous for a production, didn't she?" Rachel reminded them rather dreamily. "We wouldn't have to worry about paying for a hall, or having enough room for a decent audience, either."

Jason gave a loud cough, snatching off his soot-streaked glasses and wiping them on the edge of his jacket. "It's a nice idea, Ratchet," he said, "as long as nobody tries mucking things up for us."

"Oh, don't start all that again, Jason!" pleaded Scott wearily. "We've had horses whinnying, people crying, and goodness knows what else, but we've always found a reason for it! And those hoof marks round the back prove there's been a real horse here, not a ghost!"

"I'm not talking about a horse. Remember Rachel picking up that bookmark with the French girl's name on it? Well, it's wrong."

"Wrong?" echoed Oliver. "What do you mean wrong?"

"I thought it should be Marie *De* Ville, not Marie *Du* Ville, and I was right! I got my brother to check it for me, just to make sure!"

"Maybe that's only the way it was written," Rachel suggested, but Jason calmly picked up a fragment of broken slate and started to write on the nearest chunk of fallen stone. "OK. But, if you write MARIE DE VILLE what does that actually read?"

"Marie De Ville ..." murmured Tina obligingly. "Marie De Ville ..."

"Marie ..." echoed Oliver. "Marie ... Mary De Ville ... Hey, I get it! Mary Deville! She's called herself after the Merrie Devil!"

"Well, that's plain daft," Scott declared, after a closer inspection. "Why should anyone do that?"

"Because it was the only thing she could think of," said Oliver. "It can't be her real name."

"The librarian wouldn't know that," added Jason soberly. "Why should she bother to check, anyway?"

"But, who is she?" Rachel persisted. "Why all this mystery? What difference does it make to anyone else whether we do this production or not?"

"John Gabriel ..." mused Jason, looking around at the bare walls, pitted with deep holes and grooves, where tools and horseshoes had once hung. But except for a flat pile of grey cinders where the fire had burned, and a wall lined with stone shelves and ledges, there appeared to be nothing much to see.

"Should be OK for storing scenery and stuff, anyhow," said Scott, with a tinge of regret, hoping somehow that he might have found some clues about the lost Whispering Chamber in the *Merrie Devil* story. He was glad when Oliver started rubbing his hands together, a sure sign that he was getting impatient to try out Rachel's stage.

"Race you round to the back!" Scott yelled, working out all the short cuts which the others didn't yet know. "Last one there sells the programmes." Rachel half expected him to be jumping out of the shadows by the time they walked on to the stage, but he was already busy testing all the sound effects.

Someone else was there. Scott could see the shadowy figure out of the corner of his eye. He took a deep breath and whirled around to challenge the intruder.

"Now!" he cried triumphantly. "What do you think — " His laughter rippled all around the room, sharing the joke with his own ginger-haired, freckled-faced reflection.

"Hey, Ollie!" he called, still laughing. "I've just worked out how the Merrie Devil gets ghosts appearing when Lord Cuthbert's in the Whispering Chamber."

"'Firefly and demons, they shall do their best. To pinch, kick, scratch and so prevent his rest!'" quoted Oliver from the stage outside. "'Such fear will stir in Cuthbert's bones With creaks and moans and cries and groans!'"

Dreyton Manor suddenly seemed all creaks and groans too, and Scott couldn't help looking up at the plaster flowers where glittering chandeliers had once hung.

"Come on out, Scotty!" Rachel was calling.

"OK," he answered, with one last look over his shoulder, reminding himself to make sure that everywhere was shut and bolted before they went home.

No sense in making it easy for anyone else to get in, he thought.

Of course, everything seemed completely different when they waited to meet Lynsey at *Marigold's* three days later.

"I spoke to the groom at Broad Oak stables yesterday," said Rachel. "He says that Dreyton Manor had quite a reputation for their horses in the olden days, just like Scotty said."

"What about props?" asked Tina eagerly. "Did you ask him?"

"Yes. Seems we'd only need a hammer, a big pair of tongs to hold the horseshoes on the anvil, a bucket — "

"And don't forget the bellows to work the fire," finished Scott, appearing from nowhere as he usually did, and dumping his school bag on the ironwork table. "Any idea what time Lynsey will be getting here?"

Another round of lemonade and two packets of biscuits

later, they were joined by Oliver and Jason, both red-faced and panting hard.

"Whew! We — we thought you might have gone," Jason puffed. "Lynsey phoned through to the shop to say she might be a bit late. She's supposed to be seeing somebody from the council."

Rachel set her glass down with a loud clatter.

"That means *The Merrie Devil of Dreyton* must be on the official programme," she said, eyes alight with pleasure. "Good old Lynsey!"

Nobody minded waiting after that, although it was hard to pretend not to notice the tables being wiped down and the chairs stacked away.

"Going to be much longer, love?" the woman enquired at last, eyeing the last dregs of Scott's lemonade just as a voice boomed out from the tearoom.

"Mary! You're wanted on the telephone!"

"Come on, let's go," muttered Oliver, seeing the woman bustling away. "Lynsey won't be turning up, now."

They all crept out, past the lace curtains and the dainty tea-tables.

"Yes, sir, you've just managed to catch them," Mary was saying, reaching out one podgy hand to grab at the sleeve of Jason's school blazer. "They're here, this minute."

"Waiting for Lynsey Ronald from Studio Workshop, are you? Well, she says can you go at once to Dreyton Manor."

"Dreyton Manor?" repeated Oliver, looking around at the others. "Did she say why?"

"Sorry, love, I'm only passing the message from the policeman who's at the place right now. He's just called through on his car radiophone."

Nine

They could see the police car was still parked outside Dreyton Manor — along with a red van, a lorry with DREYTON COUNCIL painted on the side, and a green sports car, which Oliver immediately recognized.

"Oh, no," he groaned. "Look who's here, Jason."

"Might have known he'd be somewhere around!" growled Scott, all of them ignoring the bewildered way Tina looked from one to the other, whispering: "Who? Who are you talking about?"

"So kind of the police and representatives of the council to come along," a deep voice wavered towards them. "But, Lynsey dear, how did they know I'd be here?"

"Dreyton Council would like you to advise on all the safety checks, Peter," she sighed patiently. "Emergency exits, fire precautions, security, and everything else that needs to be settled."

"Not until that hoarding's been fixed round the side," someone else rapped out. "Looks like a flaming horse has trampled it down, that it does. Mindless vandalism, I call it."

They walked on in silence, wondering what on earth was going on.

"Well, it had nothing to do with my drama students," they heard Lynsey insist. "Apart from being at school, the police have already said that they were waiting for me at *Marigold's* coffee shop."

"That's right Lynsey," Oliver called out, feeling that somebody ought to start defending themselves. "Er — evening, Mr Smith."

"Albany-Smith, if you don't mind," came the haughty reply.

"What's the beef, then?" Scott wanted to know. Albany-Smith gave a refined shudder.

"I asked the council if we could use Dreyton Manor for our rehearsals, as I promised," Lynsey began hastily. "Well, they agreed, and — "

"But, didn't they say something about safety checks?" quavered Albany-Smith, vaguely shaking his silvery head. "I'm sure I recall somebody mentioning it …"

"Quite right, sir," one of the policemen assured him, busy writing in his notebook. "But that was before someone reported the hoarding being damaged, saying they'd seen some youngsters hanging around."

Oliver was immediately suspicious. "Who was it?" he demanded. "Someone trying to make trouble for us?"

"Just like a flaming horse has kicked it in!" repeated a big man in blue overalls. "Take a look for yourselves!"

They followed him across the courtyard in silence, and were amazed by the splintered layers of wood and great, jagged holes in the hoarding, now bulging out into the street, red paint and mud splattered everywhere.

"No chance of you coming here till that lot's repaired," said the man with sorry satisfaction. "Could take weeks," he added.

"Only needs a bit of patching-up!" Scott objected, with the air of somebody used to fixing bits of scenery. "My dad and Uncle Mike could do it between them, double quick."

"Only looks worse than it is because the place is in a bit of a mess, already," agreed Jason, glad to see the workman was taken aback. "We could tidy most of this between us."

"So that's settled, is it?" Albany-Smith broke in, before the workman could open his mouth again. "I was rather hoping it was time for this safety inspection to begin."

Even Rachel had to smile. Albany-Smith might seem absent-minded and a bit of a muddler — but he always managed to get things done in the end.

Who else, she wondered, would have got two burly policemen, a fire inspector and a crochety old council workman scurrying around, whilst he sauntered about giving orders?

"No horses in the stables, today?" he enquired, and nobody dared point out that it was the blacksmith's forge — now with the muddy ground even more churned up to hide the last of the hoof-prints, Scott noticed.

Dreyton Manor was vast, far bigger than they had expected, a maze of corridors, half ruined alleyways and passages leading to enormous rooms open to the sky.

Great staircases which had once wound and curled their way from floor to floor now rose only a few feet, before becoming blackened and splintered, littered with mounds of rubble, and slabs of stonework.

"Wish we had some sort of map!" Rachel complained. She was getting tired of stepping around piles of fallen bricks and squeezing through shattered doorways.

"Don't think there ever was one," smiled one of the policemen. "Or if there was, it was probably burnt in the fire, along with everything else. If some of the treasures had been saved, so would the manor."

"Treasures?" said Rachel. "What sort of treasures? Chests buried underground or hidden in secret hidey-holes, that kind of thing?"

"No, nothing quite so exciting. More like furniture, paintings, crystal chandeliers, and anything else that might have raised enough money to get the place ship-shape."

"Well," said the fire inspector at last, "most of the grounds are safe enough, but the same can't be said for the old house." The police nodded gravely. "We would need to be sure that the drama group would be closely supervised on that score."

"We're more interested in using the garden terrace for an open air theatre," Lynsey smiled eagerly, stepping aside so that Scott could fold back the wooden shutters. "Plus this one room backstage, if possible."

The moment the French windows were opened, Albany-Smith stepped out to take centre stage, striding back and forth two or three times.

"Ideal for any audience," he proclaimed, extending a hand towards the mass of overgrown grass and thistles. "That's what I shall tell the council." He turned to Scott. "And you can get that frightful hoarding repaired. Shall we say, by the end of this week?"

"Eh?" Scott wished he hadn't spoken quite so airily about his dad mending the hoarding, now. The only consolation was that the bossy council workman had run out of objections.

"So glad I was able to help," beamed Albany-Smith, strolling towards the sports car, his silky-looking jacket flung over one shoulder. "I wish you luck with your Merrie Devil."

Seeing him take off his jacket made Tina realize how warm and sunny it still was. Instinctively she raised her head, in time to see the familiar grey mane and tail mellow into shining gold, then darken to cold stone.

She listened for the sound of whinnying. Instead, it was the sudden squawking and flapping of black wings which made her jump.

"Those jackdaws, again!" came Jason's voice. "Wonder what's set them off this time?"

"Well, it can't have been horses, or we'd have found them," said Rachel. "We must have been over every part of the manor that's left standing by now. Unless they've gone the same way as the Whispering Chamber."

"That proves those horse noises came from the old forge," nodded Oliver. "Where Scotty found those hoof-prints!"

"Yes," replied Jason quietly, still not quite convinced. There had been no footprints by the forge, he remembered – so had the animal been ridden, or led? How and where had it got in? And what about the workman saying that the hoarding had been "kicked in by a flaming horse"? And from inside the grounds, too, hadn't Oliver noticed?

"Rotten hoarding!" Scott burst out bitterly, following Jason's glance. "Trust us to get lumbered with putting that lot right!"

Scott's bitterness was shortlived, however, because his dad said be wouldn't mind patching up a bit of hoarding if it meant "keeping the kids out of mischief".

"Think you can manage it by Friday, Mr Melvin?" asked Lynsey. "We'd be able to pay you something for your trouble."

"Shouldn't be a big job from what Scott says," he predicted, giving his son a friendly whack with a rolled-up newspaper. "And as long as it puts my firm in the council's good books, and we get some help with clearing away the rubbish, I'll be well pleased."

So, directly after school the following day, everyone was back at Dreyton Manor, carting away the rubble and the splinters of plywood, tidying up as much of the mess as they could.

All the time, the sound of hammering and sawing and banging thudded in their ears, but nobody complained – although Rachel couldn't help being glad when the last few daubs of mud and paint had been scrubbed away, and the rubbish loaded into the builder's van.

"Well," said Uncle Mike, standing back a little, "that's no work of art, but I'd like to see anyone getting through now.

"We've put double thickness wood all the way round the bottom edge, just to make sure."

"The manor seems like ours, again," said Tina solemnly, with a last look round. "Yesterday, it didn't feel ... it didn't feel – right, somehow ..."

"I know what you mean," Rachel smiled. "Hey, did I tell you, we're starting riding lessons again at Broad Oak stables? So I should be able to collect the props, ready for the Saturday workshop rehearsal."

"And Scott's already sorting out all the boxes and things to make the anvil and the front of the blacksmith's forge," said Tina. "And Jason's helping Oliver to write the missing bits of the script with Lynsey. I'm the only one with nothing to do."

"Grab the chance to learn your lines for the part of Firefly," came Lynsey's voice. "You won't get much time later on."

"Surprise, surprise!" grinned Rachel, slipping her arm through Tina's and trying to hurry her along. "You were bound to get the part, with your acrobatics and dancing and all that."

She was still smiling as her father drove her to the stables next day, remembering Tina's button mouth and green eyes widening at Lynsey's decision.

"I'm glad the academy's arranged some riding sessions, at last," Mr Oldham was saying, driving through gates where the sign "BROAD OAK STABLES" creaked in the breeze. "Apparently, the horses are at full strength, now, and – "

But Rachel was more interested in waving to the groom leading out two of the horses. He nodded towards Rachel and smiled.

" 'Morning, Rachel! What did your drama group think of the props I lent you? I guessed you picked them up from my shed."

"*What?*" Rachel could only stand quite still in amazement. "But — but I was just going to ask you for them. I haven't been anywhere near your shed."

"Well, that's where I put them. And they aren't there now, that's certain."

"Funny thing, though …" he added. "I was sure I'd locked the shed. And I didn't think I'd used up the paint, either."

Rachel felt her mouth go dry. "It wouldn't be — red paint, by any chance?"

"That's right, miss," he nodded. "The stuff I use to mark all our tools and riding tackle. Any idea where it's gone?"

"Not yet, I don't," said Rachel grimly, looking down at her hands, raw from scrubbing the whole evening before. "But I'm jolly well going to find out."

Ten

Although Rachel had spoken boldly enough to the young groom at Broad Oak Stables, she had to admit that she didn't quite know what to do next.

The Merrie Devil of Dreyton had given them so much to think about already, she reflected. The strange secrets of an old house – a house with its own haunted Whispering Chamber, if the story of John Gabriel the blacksmith had any truth in it!

Then, there had been this "Marie Du Ville" finding the long-forgotten script. And who could have damaged the hoarding at Dreyton Manor, then reported it to the police? The same person who had taken the tools, along with the tell-tale red paint?

Again and again, Rachel kept asking herself the same questions, never getting the right sort of answers. And while she was trying to decide whether or not to say anything to the others, the play had slowly begun to take shape.

The whole of Studio Workshop loved the idea of *The Merrie Devil of Dreyton*, from the moment Lynsey asked Oliver and Jason to outline the plot. Everyone was sure of a decent part, so they were keen to do it well, with no arguments or wounded feelings.

As expected, Oliver had been cast as John Gabriel, with the part of Squire Melrose being taken by tall, hefty-looking Daniel.

Enough of this, let me the case decide!
The bravest man – Mathilda is his bride!

His voice sounded deep and loud, feet stamping across the Parish Hall in Jason's green wellingtons. Lynsey always insisted that they rehearse in as much costume as possible, right from the very beginning. As well as getting them used to their stage clothes, she also maintained it helped actors "feel the part".

The stuffy Parish Hall did none of them any favours, Rachel considered dolefully. The walls had a habit of swallowing up words, making them seem so dull and lifeless that Daniel looked a bit ridiculous, marching around the play-group equipment and making the floor-boards squeak. She could see Lynsey frowning at those waiting their turn, trying to stop all the fidgets and the whispers.

"All right, Suzy! Try the introduction to the play by Mother Goose."

"'Fairy-land friends!'" Suzy began, after some prompting.

Fairy-land friends, come help with the tale
Of our Merrie Devil, John Gabriel!
In fighting the wrong, he sees justice done!
The scene is at Dreyton, where shines the bright sun!

Suzy tried to go on, but it was hard to concentrate with the growing babble of conversation outside.

"Can't we go over to Dreyton Manor again?" Sara pleaded, as Suzy stumbled to the end. "It's stopped raining, hasn't it?"

"Just about," said Oliver, glancing up at the high window, longing to step on to a real stage with space enough for everybody. "How much longer before we get the final OK from the Council, Lynsey?"

"Fairly soon, I hope. Then once the garden room's been checked, we'll have plenty of cover in bad weather." She sighed at a bulging dustbin liner being pushed through the door. "Looks like the Young Wives don't believe in wasting time, anyway."

They folded their scripts, hurriedly packing away costumes and props, whilst the jumble sale was set out all around them.

"We're always the ones who get pushed out," complained Robert, struggling with the ties on his miller's apron. "I'm fed up with it!"

"Never mind, Rob," said Daniel. "Nobody interrupts at Dreyton Manor."

"Bit too quiet, though," added Robert, in a bad mood that morning. "It only needs the wind moving a few branches or a bird flying out of a bush, and you'd think somebody was watching."

"Gets you used to a live audience though, doesn't it?" laughed Scott, winking around at the cluster of grinning faces. "Come on, you old moaner, what about giving me and Jason a hand with these bits of hardboard for the scenery?"

It was quite a strange procession which threaded its way through the crowded High Street, along by the clock tower and across the road to the manor. A few people paused in the middle of their Saturday shopping, some staring, others smiling as Scott lead the way like a chirpy sparrow, whistling and swinging his free arm.

"Not so bad, now that Lynsey's got the keys to the back gates," Jason commented, watching her lift the enormous padlock. "Whew, I'll be glad to dump this lot."

"OK, let's leave it just inside the gates," ordered Scott, and set the hardboard down thankfully. "We'll move it round to the old forge later on."

"An old forge?" Emma echoed. "You mean, where a blacksmith used to work?"

"That's right!" Scott nodded. Emma whirled around towards Alice and Suzy, a gleam of triumph on her face. "I said I heard a horse making a noise last time we were here, didn't I? And you all said it was the wind, or something."

"Well, we couldn't see it!" Suzy retorted. Scott was about to ask her something when Lynsey tapped him on the shoulder. "Any idea what's happened to the curtains I left here last week, Scott? I only brought them to cover up some of those props in the big cardboard box, but they seem to have vanished."

"Maybe something else was put on top," Scott suggested warily. He was still thinking about what Emma had said.

"What about the things for the blacksmith, Rachel?" asked Tina as Oliver took the stage. "Did the stables say when we could borrow them?"

"Er — not exactly," Rachel had to turn her head away, but was saved an explanation as Oliver started the scene. "Listen for your cue, Tina," she whispered, "you were great, last time."

The sun lays his head on the pillow, the ocean,
'Tis time that Firefly attend to me, here!
Awake, or in bed — make haste! Pay devotion!
The Merrie Devil, John Gabriel, bids you appear!

Everyone gasped as Tina cleared the stage with one magnificent leap, landing at Oliver's feet in a cackle of wild laughter.

Merrie master, I obey!
And at your bidding, speed my way!
Shall I enter Old Meanie's cot?
Bewitch the coins in the miser's pot?

Or attack Dame Back-Bite's tongue?
With bite of wasp, shall she be stung?

"Be great with a few loud bangs and some coloured lights flashing on and off," breathed Scott, stepping into a tall, black shadow cast by one of the broken towers and becoming half-hidden in the dim light. It would be easy to make a demon or a spook appear on stage, he thought. How could he blame anyone for thinking they could hear horses, when Dreyton Manor always seemed to put terrific ideas in their heads?

Good morrow, Edwin, A job for you to do!
My father's horse has dropped a shoe!
But to the squire, John Gabriel is gone this day!
Might I assist, and speed him on his way?

"Another set of blacksmith's tools needed there, Scott!" Lynsey cut in, snapping her fingers. "What are you doing, lurking in the shadows?" She didn't wait for an answer. "OK, so Edwin is standing in for the Merrie Devil. That's the bit which we haven't finished writing, yet, so just come right across stage and carry on, from — "

Noble master, I will do this deed!
To the Whispering Chamber, we shall proceed!

The shadows became shorter, moving around as the sun climbed the sky, warming the grey walls.

The broken towers and archways, the chipped flag-stones, the bare rafters — even the spiders' webs lacing the tangled hedges — it was all as Tina imagined when she had first seen the golden horse from her bedroom window. Only now, the manor was real and alive, as much a part of the play as they were.

John Gabriel's words had come alive for them, too. Tina hardly remembered it was Oliver speaking.

Firefly! Firefly! Come! Appear!
The Merrie Devil of Dreyton bids you draw near!

The rehearsal was hard work, the first time they had tried going through the whole production, reading through the actions when it came to the scenes which had yet to be written as best they could.

And if doors creaked and slammed, if windows rattled and hinges groaned — well, what did it matter?

Dreyton Manor belonged to them, now. With tall, stately arches, splendid French windows and trees which moved and whispered to them in the wind, the cardboard cut-outs and plastic flowers of the Parish Hall were well and truly forgotten.

Nobody really wanted rehearsal to end, but Lynsey said she had to take the younger ones back to the Parish Hall, where their mums and dads would be coming to pick them up as usual.

"All right if I leave you lot to lock up and put everything away, Oliver?" she asked, handing him a bunch of keys. "I'll collect them at the next rehearsal."

It was very quiet when they had all gone. The rumble of traffic, birds trilling away, a powerful jet aircraft roaring high above — everything sounded very faint, very far away.

"Best shift this hardboard, I suppose," said Scott at last, stooping down by the back gates. "Got the other end, Jason?"

Rachel and Tina struggled behind, carrying a supermarket carton between them which overflowed with odd bits of material, one or two wigs, scraps of fur, and old hats for "wardrobe" to sort out.   It felt very cold inside the old forge, even though the stone floor and the walls seemed quite dry.

"A – a horse ..." gasped Jason, darting towards the doorway. "It's definitely a horse this time, outside in the grounds!"

"No, Jason!" Rachel screamed after him, hands over her ears. "Can't you hear, it's inside somewhere!"

Tina had dashed out after Jason, desperately looking around and backing away from the old forge as far as she dared.

"Rachel's right! There's nothing out here! Nothing ..." Jason froze. He and Tina stood quite still, like frozen images on a film.

"What's up, now!" bellowed Oliver, almost pushing Rachel out of the way. "Can you see the horse?"

Jason had to swallow hard before he could answer. "No. No, we can't. What's more we can't hear it, even though you can. But there's something else instead ..."

"Somebody crying ..." added Tina, very nearly crying herself. "Oh, where is it coming from? What's happening?"

"Right!" Oliver finally managed to bundle Rachel out of the forge, looking pale and shaken. "We've all heard the horse, and now we can all hear the crying." He listened again, just to make sure. "That proves it's nobody's imagination, and it isn't the wind or anything like that."

He pulled out Lynsey's keys, his mouth set in the determined line which they all knew so well. "Know something?" he said. "Either somebody's been playing a whole load of tricks, trying to get rid of us, or there's more behind this than we know about. The thing is, how do we get to the truth?"

"Just a minute, Ollie," broke in Jason, just as they were all trying to get their breath back. "Where's Scotty?"

Eleven

"Keep searching!" Oliver cried out, over and over again. "He must be around somewhere!"

"You've been saying that for ages," Tina reminded him miserably, blinking hard to stop herself from crying. "Oh, what's happened to him? One minute we were all together, and the next — "

"I wouldn't put it past him to be hiding somewhere, ready to spring out and scare us all to death," interrupted Rachel darkly. "We all know what Scotty's like."

"Getting ready to play one of his jokes," said Oliver, but he and Jason were beginning to look really worried. "We were feeling uptight, anyway, hearing that horse galloping around, then somebody wailing ... One of Scotty's tricks would be pretty feeble after all that."

"Wonder what's happened to them?" said Jason, peering around the silent forge. "The horse and whoever was crying, I mean. D'you reckon Scotty went to look somewhere? He knows the manor grounds better than any of us."

"He would have come back, or shouted across, or done something when he heard us calling for him," sobbed Tina. "What if he's trapped down an old well, or fallen into a dungeon, or — "

"There's the old coal cellar," Oliver interrupted suddenly, remembering the time he and Scott had tried finding the Whispering Chamber. "That door at the bottom of the steps beside our stage, Jason!"

They soon found that Dreyton Council had been there before them and replaced the broken lock with a gigantic iron bolt and padlock. For a few moments, Oliver stood rattling the bunch of keys Lynsey had given him, knowing all the time that Scott could not possibly have got in.

A cold shiver crept down his back. What about the coal-hole which Scott had shown him? If he had fallen down that, straight on to a stone floor ...

He scrambled up the steps again, almost knocking down Jason before kicking around among the tangled grass, where he thought the coal-hole might be, still shouting, "Scott! Scotty, where are you?" then leaping up on to the stage so that he could see any holes in the ground that much easier.

"I don't see how he could have got back inside the manor," said Jason, squinting hard through his glasses. "Even that titchy window you and Scott found has been boarded up."

"The forge," Oliver repeated thoughtfully. "That's the last place where Scotty was with us, when we were putting the gear away. Did you see him come out?"

"No ... No, can't say I did. But then we were all getting in a real panic over those spooky noises, weren't we, and — "

But Oliver was already racing around the side of the stage and across the courtyard, with Jason hot on his heels. A piercing scream behind them stopped them in their tracks. "Rachel," panted Oliver, and they ran back to where they had left her, just in time to see a great cloud of dust and the swish of a black cloak in front of their eyes.

"A black horse!" said Rachel, "It — it seemed to come out of nowhere!"

"It's gone now ..." said Jason, putting an arm around Rachel. "But we still don't know how it got out, or where it's heading ..."

"Or where it came from," finished Oliver, green eyes

searching for one last glimpse, as if to make quite sure what it was he had seen.

"It-it came out of nowhere," said Rachel again, biting her lip. "Just sort of appeared, and then vanished, like a — a — "

"Like a horse being ridden away, that's what!" said Oliver firmly. "We all saw it, we know it's real, and — " He stopped, looking around again. "Did you hear a voice, just then, listen!"

"Only the leaves and the grass rustling, as usual," pronounced Jason at last, although Oliver thought he didn't sound too sure about it.

"Everyone start shouting for Scott again," he instructed. "If a horse can hide itself, then appear out of the blue, I know he can."

"Scotty! Scotty! Where are you, Scott?" Wherever he was, they knew he just had to hear them, the way they were all yelling together at the tops of their voices. So, why didn't he answer?

"Scott!" Jason called into the empty forge, then turned around again. "Hey, Ollie have you noticed that our voices don't echo in here? Why's that, I wonder?"

"Scott!" yelled Oliver, venturing further inside. "Echoes a bit more just here, Jason. Maybe you were too near the door."

"So, why have the echoes gone again, when I'm right near this wall? Remember what Scott said, when we were talking about voices echoing in some places and not in others, about thick walls, the way places were built, and — "

"Jason!" The voice sounded so faint, he wondered if he had really heard it ... But, yes there it was again, just a bit louder, this time, like somebody speaking on a bad line over the telephone.

"Jason! Jason, I can just about hear you!"

"Over here, Oliver! It's Scott! He sounds OK!"

"Where are you, Scotty?" yelled Oliver, his voice echoing again. "Can't you tell us?"

"Is Ollie there?" It was obvious that Scott hadn't heard him, although he was right next to Jason, listening hard. "Jason, where have you gone?"

"Still here!" Jason bellowed for all he was worth, Rachel and Tina cramming themselves into the space near the end of the forge, their terror at seeing the black horse giving them the power to shout as loudly as the boys.

Together they yelled until their throats ached, sometimes hearing Scott, sometimes not. At times his voice sounded strong and close at hand, other times faint and distant. It was very frustrating, but as long as there was the chance that he could hear them, they had to keep trying.

At least, Oliver comforted himself, he hadn't fallen down any coal-holes. He didn't relish the idea of going to the police and telling them what had happened although he knew that's what would have to be done if Scotty wasn't found soon.

He was just beginning to consider how to break the news to the others, when the walls of the forge began shuddering again, this time with a banging noise which got louder and louder, until it seemed to be right overhead, just as the horse's hooves had been. Then, Scott's voice, strong and clear.

"Right! If you're still in the forge, each stand in the middle of a wall and yell, all together! Wait, and I'll tell you who I can hear best!"

"Scott!" they all yelled together, at a signal from Oliver. "Scott!"

"Jason!" Scott shouted back, after a pause. "I can hear Jason!"

Yet, his shouts were completely lost on Rachel, standing

nearest the door, and Oliver had to wave her back inside so that she knew what was happening.

"Right!" Scott actually sounded as if he was quite enjoying himself. "Now, when I heard those horse noises, I was right at the end of the forge, OK? Up against the wall with all the shelves and the ledges there's something that looks like a cupboard without any door, see it? Well, it looks like solid wall, but you can get behind it. And then it leads into a sort of passage."

"I'll go and see," said Oliver, wisely barring the others with an arm outstretched in front of them. "You can all stay here, and listen to what Scotty says next. Then, come over one at a time, with Jason last."

"It's not really much of a passage," Scott continued shouting, "but make sure that whoever's last doesn't lose the end of it, same as I did. There's not all that much light up here."

"But where *is* he?" Tina wanted to know, following Oliver through the cupboard space then turning sharp right into the passage. She could feel smooth, rounded cobbles beneath her feet, resting a hand against one wall to keep her balance as she moved slowly along.

"It's fairly steep," she called back to Rachel. "Seems to be winding up and up, as well ..."

"Like the haunted house in a fairground," snapped Rachel, tense and bad-tempered now that the fright of seeing the strange black horse was beginning to wear off. "Trust Scotty to land us with something like this."

"Bit of light, just ahead," announced Oliver. "Another part of the manor where the roof's caved in, I think, so be careful. Hey, looks like a great big room twice the size of the one at the back of our stage."

"Where's Scott?" Tina cried out, trying to see clearly. "Are we in the right place?"

"'Course you are!" Scott emerged from the shadows across a flat, tiled floor, grinning as broadly as ever. "Whew, it's great to see you all again. I must've walked around a dozen times, trying to find the end of the passage. Not often I get lost, is it?"

"But, where *are* we, Scott?" persisted Oliver, looking around helplessly.

Scott gave one of his maddening grins, a sure sign that he was pleased with himself about something.

"Can't you guess, Ollie?" He paused, clearly savouring every word he was going to say, waiting to see the expressions on their faces.

"It's the squire's Whispering Chamber."

Twelve

"Well," Scott burst out impatiently, "isn't anybody going to say something? I thought you'd all be pleased."

"How do you know this is the Whispering Chamber, Scotty?" asked Oliver, at last. "It — well, it doesn't look anything special."

"What can you expect when a place has been standing empty for years and years? 'Course this is the Whispering Chamber. How come there are so many different special sound effects that work from here, and nowhere else in Dreyton Manor? That's why everyone though it was haunted. And that's why it's in the story of the Merrie Devil."

Scott sounded so sure of himself, nobody could think of anything to say. The daylight filtering through the broken rafters reached only one corner of the enormous room, the part where they now stood, grouped together. Dusty floorboards and high walls stretched away into a black darkness, broken only by a few patches of light shining on thick cobwebs, a rusty grating, a length of picture rail — and a wooden horseshoe, set into one wall, Tina noticed.

Rachel was sure she could feel a mouse scampering around somewhere dangerously near her feet, shrinking back into the gloom as far as she dared.

"Come on, let's go home," she pleaded, with a shiver. "We've had enough frights for one day, and I don't want any more!"

"Frights?" said Scott at once. "Oh, you mean thinking I'd gone missing, or something, then hearing me making all those noises in the old forge — like this?"

"Scott, don't!" cried Tina, hands over her ears as a slow, mournful-sounding tattoo echoed and re-echoed throughout the room, reaching every unseen corner. "Th-that sounds horrible."

"Bet it sounds great down in the old forge, though. Like a ghostly drummer calling an army to fight, or footsteps marching through the manor — ha-ha-ha-ha!"

Scott's special, bloodcurdling laugh was even more frightening, floating away into the darkness, then coming back at them, from every direction, nearer and nearer, until one burst of laughter seemed like a hundred.

Rachel screamed, her cries adding to the noise, but seeming more real, and close at hand. It was uncanny how sounds could be the same, and yet different at the same time.

"OK, Scotty, we believe you," Jason told him, striding across and making a grab for his arm. "Now, pack it in, and let's get out of here. We will come back with a few torches, and have a really good look round."

"Eh?" Scott was torn between surprise and indignation. "But, I thought you'd be itching to try lots more sound effects up here. We could record the best ones on cassette, then run a lead down to a speaker in the garden room, drape it with a black curtain to make it into our Whispering Chamber for the production, and — "

"OK, Scott," said Jason firmly. "Now, supposing you hear what happened to us?"

"Oh, yeah!" Scott sounded so excited and so cheerful, that it made everyone else feel much better — even if they were trying to keep their balance, half-slipping, half-sliding down a winding, cobbled passage. "So, what's been going on while I've been in the Whispering Chamber?"

He had to wait until they had all managed to squeeze out into the back end of the forge, grinning around at the

80

stripes of dust and dirt where they had put their hands up to their faces, before they would tell him.

"Scott Melvin presents!" he announced, snatching up Lynsey's curtain to wave with a flourish, "the Studio Workshop Tigers!"

"Give it a rest, Scotty," Rachel begged him, grabbing the curtain wearily. "We're all feeling worn out, right? And this has got to be washed – as soon as I've taken the blacksmith's things back to Broad Oak stables."

"What?"

"Look, don't all start asking questions!" she yelled, silencing the clamour of voices and stuffing everything into the nearest carrier bag. "I'll explain everything in a minute." She raised a hand to her aching head, swaying a little. Tina rushed towards her.

"We're going straight into town to get you a can of drink, and see what sandwiches they've got left, Rachel! Then I'm off to Halstead Park for a packed lunch and some fresh air for a change." She gave a brief glare in the direction of her unfortunate brother, leaving him to wonder quite what he had done to deserve it. "This lot can do what they like."

She proceeded to bustle Rachel away, leaving the boys looking sheepishly at each other.

"All right," agreed Rachel. "We'll find a pay-phone, so we can all ring home."

It was the middle of the afternoon before they finally acted on Tina's suggestion about going to Halstead Park, Oliver carrying a jumbo bottle of orange squash which the Young Wives had given them before they cleared away after their Jumble Sale.

"Poor kids!" he heard someone else saying, as they walked out into the street. "Still no sign of them getting a place of their own, is there?"

They had strolled to the park without saying much, each

wondering just what the Young Wives would say if they knew where Studio Workshop had been rehearsing — a huge, spooky old house sheltering a mysterious black horse and its cloaked rider.

Would *they* have believed it? Oliver asked himself, if it hadn't happened to them?

"Well, at least I proved how all that galloping and whinnying could be heard in the old forge," Scott pointed out. "The horse must've been somewhere near the Whispering Chamber, the same as I was."

"Did you see the horse?" Jason asked him. "Or hear it?"

"No." He could tell that Scott was doing his best to remember every detail. "I didn't. But you saw for yourselves how you can hear things in some parts and not in others, didn't you? That chamber is a massive place, don't forget."

"So how would the horse reach it, Scotty?" persisted Oliver. "D'you reckon there's another way in?"

"Must be. Nobody's going to have a great big room like that with only a narrow little passage leading down to the forge, are they? Can you imagine the butler or whoever it was bringing up the trays when the squire wanted something to eat in there?"

"Or the maids carrying up all the bedclothes if anyone like Edwin or Lord Cuthbert had to stay the night," added Tina, pleased when they all started to laugh. "So why is the passage there, then? John Gabriel must have been an important person."

"Lynsey said he probably was," put in Rachel rather gravely, folding an empty crisp packet into tiny squares. "He had a play written about him, didn't he? And what about Tina's golden horse, and all those horseshoe carvings we found at the manor, and the model of him and his forge at Felbourne Museum? That bit of the story fits together."

"What about the black horse?" said Oliver. "Does that fit into the story of the Merrie Devil, as well?"

"I know one thing," said Rachel at last. "Somebody took the pincers and the tongs from Broad Oak stables, and left them in the forge at the manor. The red paint that was splashed around the broken hoarding — remember? The same person used Lynsey's bit of curtaining to wipe some of it away. That came from Broad Oak stables, as well. Charlie the groom told me. It's what he uses to mark all his tools."

Silently, Scott unwrapped the tools from the curtain, setting them out carefully on the park bench. The initials "B.O.S." were clear to see on the inside of the pincers, but the bottom half of the tongs were smeared with red, as though someone had been in a great hurry to paint over them.

"I — I know I should have said something when the tools went missing," Rachel admitted with another sigh. "But, honestly, I didn't see what any of us could do about it. Of course, I recognized the red paint, but there was nothing else that made any sense."

"These stables where you go, Ratchet," said Oliver suddenly. "We could go there, couldn't we — all together, I mean?"

"Of course we could." Rachel looked up in surprise. "Broad Oak's open seven days a week."

"OK, then!" Oliver stood up firmly, gathering up the last of the cakes ready to throw to the ducks. "That's where we'll be going tomorrow. Let's hear what your friend Charlie the groom has to say about all this."

Thirteen

They only just managed to catch the bus which ran every hour from Dreyton to Willoughby Park, stopping near Broad Oak Stables.

Scott and Tina's mother had made it clear she was in two minds about letting them go, only relenting when they promised faithfully to be back before teatime.

"And don't come home in the same state as you did yesterday!" she had scolded. "Leaving it until the last minute before telephoning to say you're going to be late. You'd think Oliver Davis and that nice Rachel Oldham would know better."

Mrs Oldham hadn't been too keen, either.

All night long, Rachel had tossed and turned in bed, hearing hooves pounding towards her, then shouting about black horses, and waking herself up.

"Are you sure you have got to go out with your friends from Studio Workshop this afternoon, darling?" her mother had enquired gently, stroking a length of fair hair back from Rachel's forehead. "I think you've been working much too hard on this production about the Merrie Devil black-smith."

Quite a joke, that was, Rachel conceded wryly, settling back in her seat and chewing one of Tina's favourite wine gums.

They were all enjoying the ride out of town, with the bus chugging its way up the narrow hill, chestnut trees just about to break into blossom on either side. The day was warm enough for most of the windows to be wound down, a deliciously refreshing breeze fanning their faces and lifting their hair.

The broken towers and dark passages of Dreyton Manor seemed far away, with only the hum of traffic on the motorway reminding them that it was still really there, like somebody waiting at home.

Through the window, Tina could just see one side of the old house, the side facing the broken fence where Scott had first led them inside.

The horse could not have left the manor grounds that way, she knew, so there must be another way out. But where else could it have gone?

She tried picturing the horse in her mind, comparing it to the stone horse at Dreyton Manor — the shape of the head, the broad back, the sleek lines of the tail ...

She had the feeling there was something different about the black horse, something she had seen, almost without knowing it.

"That black horse must be the link between Dreyton Manor and Broad Oak Stables," Oliver was saying, bending down to check the tools in his schoolbag. "And whoever was riding it yesterday must have been the person who took this gear and left it in the old forge."

"And," he continued, taking a deep breath, "as for the red paint — "

"No shoes!" Tina broke in suddenly. "Now, I remember. There weren't any shoes."

"Tina, what are you talking about?" demanded Scott with a short laugh. "Who didn't have any shoes?"

"The black horse! I *knew* I'd seen something missing. The black horse didn't have any horseshoes."

All eyes were on Tina, Rachel hearing again the sound of hooves thundering towards her through the night, becoming louder, yet strangely hollow.

"Don't forget, Tina," she said quietly, "we only saw the horse for a few seconds."

85

"It didn't have any horseshoes," Tina repeated, yet again. "Honestly, it didn't. I knew, as soon as I saw it again in my mind, galloping up this hill."

"That means it's being ridden over fields and grass, not roads and bridle paths," commented Rachel. "And it isn't being kept in proper stables, either, otherwise it would be shod properly, the same as all the other horses."

Nothing much was said after that. None of them had really expected to find the black horse happily cantering around at Broad Oak Stables. But they had thought that someone there might know something about the horse, and why it had been seen at Dreyton Manor.

"Broad Oak!" the driver bellowed up at them. "You kids getting off?"

It was only a short walk to the stables, along a winding path from where they could see some riders exercising their horses. Every so often, one or two would pull gently at the reins, stopping to admire the views across the hills towards Dreyton.

"Hi, Rachel!" One of the riders cantered up to them, a young man in a very smart tweed jacket and black riding hat. "Come to show your friends around? Sorry all the horses are out, but it's such a nice afternoon."

"You're the one we've come to see, Charlie! Want to know what happened to those tools which disappeared out of your shed?"

"Charlie!" Tina burst out. "Are you Charlie the groom?" The way Rachel spoken, she had imagined somebody a lot older.

Charlie grinned, swinging one leg across the saddle, and jumping down easily. He led the horse forward a few paces, rubbing the blaze of white down its long, velvety nose.

"Now," he said, "what's all this about my spare set of tools?"

He stood, watching Oliver putting his schoolbag on the stump of a tree, so that Rachel could unwrap them from the curtain and set them out in a row.

"Well, I'll be jiggered!" Charlie said at last, picking up the tongs, his warm country burr becoming more noticeable every minute. "But who's tried painting over the handles?"

"The same person who left them at Dreyton Manor," Oliver told him grimly. "That's where we found them, yesterday, when we were packing away our props."

"Props?" For a moment, Charlie looked bewildered. Then he jabbed a finger at Oliver, and gave another grin.

"I get it! You're this drama group Rachel told me about, the one that's doing a play about the blacksmith over at Dreyton."

"That's us," Jason nodded. "But we aren't the ones who borrowed your tools behind your back. And we didn't try painting the handles, either."

"No?" Already Charlie seemed more than a little confused.

"No," Scott chipped in eagerly. "We reckon it was the person riding the black horse."

"The — the black horse?" Charlie took of his riding hat and wiped his forehead with the back of his hand. "Come on, Maiden," he said shortly, making a clicking noise with his tongue. "Let's leave our visitors to have a look round."

"What?" cried Oliver, all of them beginning to run to keep up with him. "Look, you can't just leave us here without saying anything, not after we've come all this way. We only want to know if there's a black horse at Broad Oak."

"Why do you want to know?"

"Because," panted Jason, "right after we found your

tools at Dreyton Manor, we saw this black horse being ridden through the grounds."

Charlie slowed down a little, looking straight ahead towards the stable block. Scott could see him swallowing hard once or twice, before he spoke again.

"So, what was it like, this black horse? Any markings? Fully grown, would you say?"

"Definitely fully grown," nodded Rachel, frowning a little.

"But it didn't have shoes," Tina put in. "Rachel says that means it's being ridden across fields."

"Either that, or someone's paring the hooves, the same as people file their nails to keep them in trim." Charlie stopped suddenly, calling to Oliver.

"I've just thought, is my file in that bag? I know I put one out for you to use in your play, only a broken old thing it were."

"No file here," announced Oliver, after they'd all rummaged inside. "And we didn't leave anything behind at the manor."

"Then," said Charlie, beginning to lead Maiden on again, "somebody's trying to look after that horse all by themselves. If they can pare the hooves, they don't have to pay no blacksmith, see? I don't know what to make of this, that I don't. And you say the horse was at Dreyton Manor? An odd thing, that is ..."

For a moment, Charlie seemed to forget they were there, his eyes on Maiden's hooves, slowly clip-clopping their way through the stable door. "It had this reputation — remember I was telling you, Rachel?"

Rachel didn't answer. She was concentrating hard on something else. Charlie was leading them along a narrow, winding passage just like the one at Dreyton Manor.

"Where are you taking us, Charlie?" Oliver asked him, staring around at the smooth brick walls.

"Only up to the top stalls. Now that we've got all the horses back, some are kept downstairs, and the rest up here. It's the sort of thing you get in lots of larger stables, especially the ones with a busy street or a pathway outside."

"Well ..." said Jason, half under his breath. "So now we know what was once at the top of that passage that led from the old forge! It must have been another stable!"

"In the Whispering Chamber?" Oliver hissed back at him. "Who'd want to lead horses up from the forge and into the Whispering Chamber?"

"The Merrie Devil?" Scott felt it was worth a guess.

"The Merrie Devil ... Yes," began Charlie. Seems that in the old days, sick horses used to be taken to him to be cured. All on account of some magic that was supposed to be at Dreyton, so folks said. I remember my grandad telling me something about it when I were a lad. My father, too."

"So, why shouldn't the black horse be seen there, then?" Scott persisted, watching Charlie closely. "And why did you walk away, just because we mentioned it?"

It was very quiet in the stable, with only the sound of Maiden whinnying gently as Charlie began brushing and combing her coat with smooth, deft strokes.

"Tell me something else," said Charlie at last. "The person riding this black horse. Could you say who it was?"

"Somebody in a long, black cloak," said Tina, shivering at the memory. "We were all pretty scared."

Very slowly, Charlie turned around to face them, looking from one to the other.

"Yes, I can imagine. I've never heard of it being seen at Dreyton before, but it's been sighted around these parts quite a few times. Midnight, folks call it, for it never appears until after sunset. I never believed it, not until I saw it with my own eyes."

"You — you've seen it?" gasped Rachel, relieved that somebody was at last taking them seriously.

"Yes, I have, more's the pity. And I'm telling you, keep well away from Dreyton Manor, for fear of seeing Midnight again. Because if you don't, all kinds of misfortune will come your way, same as everyone else who's crossed the path of the black horse!"

Fourteen

Charlie turned his back, standing close to Maiden and stroking her head.

"Misfortune?" Oliver repeated steadily. "What do you mean, Charlie? What's happened to the people who have seen the black horse?"

Charlie shook his head impatiently.

"All manner of things. First time I saw it, I drove a chisel into my hand next day. Gerda, the stablegirl who used to work here, she was called home on account of her father being took ill. And the last time it appeared at Broad Oak, half the horses went down with that virus."

Scott opened his mouth to say something, but Jason held him back.

"I think we've stayed here long enough," he murmured. "It's nearly time to catch the bus back home, anyway."

"Bye, Charlie," Tina called softly, but there was no reply.

Slowly, they made their way back down the winding cobble-stone passageway to the stable entrance, looking all around one more time.

"Come on," said Tina, taking Rachel's arm. "We don't want to miss the bus."

They left Broad Oak in silence, the sun was low in the sky and cast long pointy shadows. Not a soul was in sight. After all that Charlie had said, they felt as if the sinister black horse was somewhere near, waiting to gallop across their path.

It was only when they were on the bus home, with Broad Oak well into the distance, that they started talking properly about all that had happened.

"That black horse was real," said Oliver decidedly. "Remember those hoof marks Scotty found by the old forge? And even Charlie said that somebody must be looking after it, somewhere."

"And I reckon it's somewhere near the Whispering Chamber!" cried Scott, almost jumping out of his seat. "That's why you lot heard those horse noises in the old forge, because of the passage that leads up to the chamber, the same sort that Charlie showed us."

"But the horse couldn't have come down the passage and out of the forge," Rachel put in thoughtfully. "We were standing right outside, Tina and me."

"So, there's got to be another way in, like I've said before. And if we found that, I bet we'd find the black horse as well."

The more they thought about it, the more it seemed that Scott was right. Although none of them could explain why a cobble-stone passage should link the forge with somewhere as grand as the Whispering Chamber.

"Might have something to do with the story about the Merrie Devil helping sick horses at Dreyton," Rachel suggested. "It was probably only those echoes and sound effects inside the chamber that made people believe it was haunted, like it says in our play."

It was all beginning to make sense, even Tina had to admit that. But with Charlie's words of warning about the black horse flooding back into her mind she couldn't help feeling uneasy.

"You — you're not thinking of going back to Dreyton Manor, now, are you?" she faltered, as the broken towers came in sight. "The police, that fire inspector and the man from the council, they all said Lynsey had to be with us."

"Ok, then!" her brother retorted. "We'll get there before

the Wednesday rehearsal starts. Ollie's got to turn up early to unlock the place, hasn't he?"

The three boys worked everything out between them, walking from the bus station to the clock tower.

It would be best, they said, if Rachel and Tina arrived at the proper time, then Lynsey would probably think they were all together, as usual. Jason and Scott arranged to bring torches, and Oliver thought some chalk might be a good idea, in case they needed to mark their way.

"Don't look so worried, Tina," came Rachel's comforting voice. "If they find the answer to all the mystery about the black horse, we can really concentrate on putting on a good production."

"And if they don't?" Tina persisted, her green eyes wide and round.

"If they don't, at least we'll know Scotty was wrong. But we've got to let them find out for sure."

"Did I tell you, Mummy's given me one of her ballgowns to wear as Mathilda's wedding dress? And when I saw Shirley today, she said she'd almost finished Ollie's blacksmith costume. Quite a lucky week it's been for us, hasn't it?"

Tina was invited to tea the following afternoon, so that she could help Rachel take the greasepaints down to Dreyton Manor afterwards. And Scott's dad offered to collect all three boys from school, drive them back to load up his builder's van with the set for the forge, than take them on to rehearsal.

"We'll be nearly an hour early," Oliver grinned across the shed door, which he and Scott carried between them. They had painted it black with a silver horseshoe in the middle, and it looked most impressive. "And nobody can say anything when we've got to unload all this gear for the play."

If anything, the old manor seemed quieter than usual, every sound floating towards them in the warm afternoon. Somewhere, inside the house, a door or a window banged softly in a stray draught. The ancient bushes groaned and sighed in a sudden breeze.

They began talking in low voices, casting anxious glances behind them, as though there was a danger of being overheard by someone unseen and unknown. Nobody felt like laughing, or making jokes, now.

"I'm pretty sure there's something behind that door on the birdcage balcony," Scott muttered, looking up at the flutter of jackdaw wings. "That's about the right height from the ground for the Whispering Chamber, if you think about that passageway going up from the forge."

"I never thought of that, Scotty," confessed Oliver, craning his neck. "D'you think it's worth scouting around from this end, just in case there's some steps or a staircase leading up to it?"

"Good idea!" approved Jason. "We'll go through the forge, and then if you find the other entrance, you can give us a shout."

"Otherwise, just follow us up the passageway," finished Scott, taking a torch from his sports bag. "Here, put this in your pocket."

They hurried away, leaving Oliver staring up at the balcony and wondering where to start looking. He noticed a rim of stonework running along the wall, grimy and black, but fairly easy to pick out above the French windows and the stage. Follow that, he reasoned, along the side of the building, and, if Scotty was right, that rim went all around the outside of the Whispering Chamber.

Not daring to take his eyes off the stonework, Oliver stumbled around to the side of the stage, then as far as he could towards the front of the house.

To one side, he could just see the line of stone archways which had once held stained glass windows, where Jason had first heard the sounds of a horse. There were great gaps in the walls now, he noticed, showing that this was where the heart of the fire had been. The stonework rim he was following had become chipped and broken, blackened by the smoke and soot.

"Now," Oliver muttered to himself, casting his eyes carefully down the wall where the rim finally petered out. "If I can just work out where I am ..."

But there was no need to work anything out. Oliver knew he had found what he was looking for the moment he saw the stone shield, set with the sign of a horseshoe. It was above a small porch with a gentle slope at either side, which he could see quite clearly through a tangle of rusting ironwork, and thick creeper.

He had to get to that door, he told himself, tugging and tearing at fistfuls of whiskery green stems, until he found a piece of the ironwork which had rusted away, just wide enough for him to wriggle through.

Heart pounding, he ran towards the door. Then his thumb was on the latch, squeezing it down hard.

There was a heavy click from the other side, a creak echoing through the old house and the door groaned ajar, waiting for him to enter.

He took one step forward but no more. His own shadow on the door was blotted out by another, taller and larger, looming up behind him, and a strong hand grabbed at his shoulder, almost lifting him off his feet.

"Caught you at last, you young devil!" a rough voice shouted in his ear.

Fifteen

It was much darker inside the Whispering Chamber than Jason or Scott had imagined.

"Wasn't half this bad when we were up here last time," Scott muttered. "These torches aren't much use, either."

"That's because there's no light coming in from outside," said Jason, trying to peer ahead. "Looks like all the windows have been boarded up."

He gave one or two sharp raps with his knuckles, the knocks rumbling into a drum-roll tattoo, becoming louder and louder, then dying away.

"Jason!" Scott shouted without thinking, the walls taking up the echo.

"Jason! Jason! Jason-Jason-ason-ason-ason-son-son ..."

"I'm positive it wasn't as dark as this before," Scott grumbled again, the beam of his torch wavering around uncertainly.

"Now," he continued, still looking around, "it must be the hall and the garden room at the back of our stage that's underneath this place. But at this end, we're nearer to the front of the house. So, if we keep going forward, we should see some light coming in from the door behind that birdcage balcony — "

"Scotty!" Jason broke in, clutching his friend's arm. "Scott, stop a minute. What's that shadow, over there?"

"Over where?"

"Over there, almost straight in front. Wait a sec, and you'll see it again. I thought I'd forgotten to clean my glasses, at first."

They stood close together, holding their breath and

watching. Then Scott began tutting with impatience, half inclined to start finding his way through the darkness again.

"Hold on a bit longer," whispered Jason. "Now, look up, towards the ceiling ... "

To begin with, it was nothing more than a small triangle of light. But gradually, it spread out in front of them like a great fan, opening wider and wider, before closing up into darkness again.

Scott racked his brains, trying to think where he had seen something like it before. Then he remembered.

"It's the sun, moving across this part of Dreyton Manor, the same as when it moves across the stone horse, a bit later on. Only, there must be some clouds in the way. You watch!"

The triangle of light began spreading again, fanning out that much quicker, and with enough brightness to beam across the whole of one corner.

"Scott!" Jason whispered. "There's somebody else in here! Look! A — a whole line of faces, looking at us from behind that curtain thing!"

Scott stood still for only a moment. Then he marched as boldly as he could towards the intruders, brushing away a cloud of dust and cobwebs with a whoop of triumph.

"Fooled you! But, don't worry, I fell for the same trick, downstairs! They're mirrors!"

"Whew!" Jason gazed along the lines of fading reflections with much relief, taking off his glasses to give them a wipe, then putting them back on again. "I — I really thought — "

"So did I," grinned Scott, laying a hand on Jason's shoulder. "And that proves I was right about the way demons and ghosts were supposed to appear in the Whispering Chamber. There must be mirrors all round the walls, making it look as if there are hundreds of people in here, instead of just us two."

97

More light was filtering into the room, and they were becoming accustomed to the gloom. Scott moved forward at a much brisker pace and Jason struggled to keep up with him.

Suddenly, Scott came to a halt, glancing over his shoulder.

"Did you hear something just then, Jason? Sounded like somebody crying out ... "

"Jason, Jason, are you anywhere around?"

"Lynsey," whispered Scott, shining his torch around and moving forward at the same time. "But, where is she?"

"I keep telling you, the others aren't here."

Jason and Scott stared across at each other, their faces gleaming like wax in the yellow light of their torches.

"That's Ollie," breathed Jason. "Listen!"

"Jason and Scott aren't anywhere near here. I came early to unlock the gates and bring some stuff for our play."

"So, how is it the padlock on this porch keeps getting broken?" a man's voice demanded fiercely. "Time and again, Dreyton Council have tried locking it up, but it's forever being burst open again."

"That's nothing to do with us. We haven't even been in this part of the grounds before."

"So, what's the point of the torch in your pocket, eh?" shouted another voice.

"Don't need a torch to unload scenery and suchlike," the first man chimed in. "And you still haven't told us how this mirror got broken, neither."

"Well, none of us threw it out of any window, like you said we did!" Oliver shouted back. "Why don't you take a look at some of the scenery we've built ourselves, then you'd know we wouldn't smash anything on purpose."

"Oliver!" Lynsey broke in warningly, glancing at the irate security man and his companion. "The gentlemen have explained that the mirror came from inside the manor, because it has the old crest stamped on the back of the frame."

"Can't see what all the fuss is about," snorted Oliver, bending down to pick up one of the fragments. "The mirror's nearly worn out, and the frame's been mended with tin-tacks."

"Never mind that. What about that gate being trodden down? And the bolt being wrenched off the side door?"

"What's he on about?" muttered Jason. "Where are they, can you see?"

"How can I see, with all the windows boarded up," Scott demanded, turning his head first one way and then the other. "Can't even see where the windows are, half the time."

They stumbled on a bit further, Scott becoming more and more bad tempered, but determined not to be defeated.

"Ollie said that they were in a part of the grounds where we'd never been, somewhere with a porch. They can't mean the front proch with all the pillars, can they, because that's been chained and boarded up for ages."

"So, what do we do now? Go back down the passage to the forge?"

"What, when we've got this far? If we heard Ollie just now, we must be somewhere near that porch, and the other entrance to the Chamber!"

"But Lynsey's here. That means it's time for rehearsals."

"Can't help that, can we? And at least Oliver knows where we are."

By this time, Oliver was inside the old forge, and he couldn't help groaning aloud. The two security men had been ranting and raving the whole time they were marching him along the hall and unlocking the back door to let him and Lynsey out. Each time they paused for breath, Lynsey could only try to calm them down, telling them that Studio Workshop would put right any damage, and pointing out that they had nowhere else to rehearse. Oliver had thought they were never going to leave them alone.

And now, here he was, trying to yell a message to those two in the Whispering Chamber, and all they could say was that he knew where they were.

"Can't you hear me?" he yelled again. "Shout back if you can!"

"Oliver, what are you doing in there?" It was Shirley, coming to see what all the noise was about. "I thought you were supposed to be trying on your costume."

"Er, I — I was practising some sound effects for the play," he stammered. "What about the costume, then, Shirley?"

"Not a bad fit," she nodded, turning him around with pink, plump hands. "But you could do with something around your neck, I think. Let's see what we've got."

"No!" yelled Oliver, seeing her about to go back towards the forge. "Er, I — I think Rachel wants you to see her dress for Mathilda. She — she's bringing it, especially — "

"All right, no need to panic," Shirley smiled. "I've already had enough of that from Lynsey, wanting to know where Scott is!"

Lynsey was giving Studio Workshop what she called her "pep talk". "We're getting to the point where you should all be managing without your scripts, so don't rely on Shirley for a prompt. Next, anyone having trouble getting props, see me after rehearsal, so that we can sort things out before wardrobe next week. Now, about make-up. Rachel and Tina ... something wrong, Tina?"

"N-no," Tina shuffled her feet uncomfortably. "It — it's just, when I saw Oliver — "

"Ah, yes. Oliver," Lynsey's voice was developing the sharp edge to it which, the Studio Workshop knew only too well, meant they were in for a hard time. "And, what about Jason and Scott?"

"Er, they'll both be here soon," said Oliver, avoiding the worried expression on Tina's face.

"They both know they're needed for the scene with Lord Cuthbert and Edwin in the Whispering Chamber. All right, then." Lynsey proceeded to roll up the sleeves of her shirt, and stormed across the stage.

"Everyone taking parts of the people of Dreyton, come and watch while I make up Suzy and Robert. Then it's the second act with Firefly and the Merrie Devil. And if those two haven't turned up by then, there's going to be trouble."

"Oliver!" Rachel hissed across at him, while Lynsey tied an old teacloth underneath Suzy's chin. "What's wrong? What's happened to Scott and Jason?"

"They're still in the Whispering Chamber, aren't they?" Tina quavered. "Supposing they can't get back by the time we've finished our scene, Ollie?"

"We'll have to scrape through somehow, until they manage to show up," he told her, fingering the fragment of broken mirror. "If Scotty doesn't find his way around the Whispering Chamber now, he never will."

Rachel and Tina could tell that Oliver was upset by the way the security man had spoken to him.

"Stand by, Oliver and Tina!" announced Lynsey. "Rachel, you're on stage, starting from your speech about Edwin spending a night in the Whispering Chamber."

"Edwin I love ..." Rachel began nervously. "Edwin, I love, Cuthbert is not for me ... Yet, the-the haunted chamber ..."

"The Whispering Chamber!" Lynsey broke in, turning

around at Shirley's prompt. "Yet, the Whispering Chamber ... Come along, you can do better than this, Rachel! You're worried about your sweetheart, because if he doesn't spend the night in the Whispering Chamber ... something wrong again, Tina?"

Tina gave a loud gulp in reply, and fumbled for her handkerchief.

"I – I think I've got a bit of a cold."

"Well, don't keep looking at Oliver, as if you expect him to cure it. He's the Merrie Devil, not a doctor. Really, what with you two, Jason and Scott going off somewhere, and Rachel forgetting to act, I'm beginning to wonder if this production's going to be finished on time. Now, Oliver!"

> *There is no cause for tears, fair maid,*
> *John Gabriel comes to Edwin's aid!*
> *My faithful Firefly has the task*
> *Of doing all that I shall ask ...*

Oliver threw back his head as he spoke at first because it felt right for the part of the Merrie Devil. Then, he noticed that he could see the underside of the birdcage balcony, where, he knew, the door was wedged ajar by jackdaws nesting just inside the Whispering Chamber.

> *My servant shall work a most dread fright,*
> *Lord Cuthbert will not last the night!*

Oliver's voice carried through the gap and alerted Scott and Jason.

"Hear that?" said Jason in a loud whisper. "Ollie and Tina are both onstage."

"That means we must be getting nearer the balcony," said Scott. He gave Jason an encouraging push. "Go on,

102

keep going! Once I can get the window open a bit, we'll be able to see right inside! Move it, Jason!"

Their footsteps were echoing right through the enormous room like thunder, but Jason and Scott no longer cared, edging their way further and further in the direction of the voices, until they could see a thin chink of light, an untidy, black mass rustling near the top.

"Lynsey was right about a bird's nest jamming open the window," whispered Scott, putting one eye to the crack, before feeling around expertly for a handle or a bolt. "And I can see the balcony outside. Let's wait till all the demons jump up on the stage, so that nobody hears me giving it a push — "

"No!" The hoarse whisper travelled all around the walls, making the jackdaws start to squawk and flap their wings. "No! No! No! No-no-no-no — "

Sixteen

It was hard to tell where the voice was coming from, with
the Whispering Chamber joining in the low, desperate cry.
"No! No-no-no-no-no — "
Scott and Jason stood quite still, the words of the Merrie
Devil floating up towards them.

> *In the Whispering Chamber, such dread, such fear*
> *Shall fill all the hearts of those who draw near ...*
> *For, naught but the brave can dare win the day.*
> *The ghosts of Dreyton to send far away!*

Suddenly, the great room felt even darker, the wavering
torch beams and the chink of light from the window
seeming to draw a host of black shadows towards them,
nearer and nearer.
Then the voice again, closer this time.
"Please ... come with me ... "
Scott's hand touched a long sleeve, and he felt along from
the shoulder to the slim wrist, and the clasp of a thin bracelet.
"A — a girl!" he gasped out. "It — it's a girl!"
They were beginning to see her more closely now — a
tall, lean figure, with long, dark hair in a single, thick
plait.
"Careful when you come to this slope," she whispered.
"Part of the wall's collapsed near the door. Good thing
those men haven't fixed the bolt ... "
She had spoken without thinking, too intent on fumbling
with the old-fashioned brass latch to see Scott pointing an
accusing finger.

"So, it was *you* who yanked the bolt off the door. You must have heard Ollie getting blamed for that."

The girl began to cry, covering her face with both hands and sobbing so hard that soft-hearted Jason could hardly bear it.

"You — you are the person who's been keeping the black horse here aren't you?" he said.

She nodded in reply, still weeping.

"What about Charlie's tools from Broad Oak Stables?" Scott demanded. "And I bet it was you who smashed that hoarding and got us into another row!"

"We had to clear up after you," Jason added swiftly. "It was hard work, carting all the muck away, and scrubbing off the red paint."

"Please, d-don't say any more," begged the girl, close to tears again. "I — I know what you must think."

Scott opened his mouth, then closed it again, thinking hard.

Why shouldn't they just go and tell Lynsey, he argued? The girl hadn't thought twice about making things difficult for them. Why should they consider her feelings?

And yet, she looked so thin, so pale, with dark smudges underneath her eyes, and he could see her hands trembling as she pushed the door open.

"Domino!" she called softly. "Domino!"

The boys heard the horse whinnying in reply before it appeared, cantering towards them, the magnificent mane rippling proudly. It seemed to sense that Jason and Scott were watching, backing away a little, then pawing the ground, ears pricked forward as the girl spoke.

"It's all right, Domino. We're still together, still safe."

Scott followed her gaze around the four half-ruined walls with a ragged square of grass in the middle. This was where the fire had been at it's height, he guessed. Here, the flames

105

and the heat had been fierce enough to make the roof collapse, leaving only the rafters, stretching overhead like a bony skeleton.

"It's a great hiding place," he admitted. "No wonder we couldn't find where the horse was."

"But why did you have to come here?" she groaned miserably, burying her head against Domino's slender neck. "Why did you have to decide on a play about the Merrie Devil?"

Hearing her mention the name of their production, Jason's quick brain started working.

"Marie Du Ville ..." he murmured. "You told Felbourne Museum that you were a French student!"

"How else could I find out what you were doing? When I heard you talking about the production, I knew I had to read the script before you did."

"Look," she continued, speaking quickly, "you go back to your rehearsals, and I'll meet you afterwards. I – I promise, I will explain, and then you'll understand, I know you will. As long as it's before sunset."

"Before sunset?" echoed Jason in surprise. "Why sunset?"

But the girl only shook her head, leading them through a wooden gate lurching on its hinges, across a stretch of rubble where a room or a smaller chamber had once been, then out through the porch door which Oliver had found.

"Don't forget what I said!" she called. "Be back before sunset! Before – before he appears ..."

"What did she mean by that?" wondered Jason, blinking through his glasses.

"Search me." Scott glanced up at the sky, already streaked with pink and gold. "Shouldn't be all that long, anyway."

They hurried on, back towards the forge and the rear of the house, both feeling tired and dusty, but gratified by the grins and sighs of relief which greeted them although Lynsey gave a shriek of dismay.

"You look perfectly dreadful, both of you! What on earth have you been doing?"

"Checking a few sound effects," explained Scott, in what he considered to be a moment of brilliant inspiration. "We — we got a bit lost, Lynsey."

"Lost?" cried Lynsey in disbelief. "You?"

"Easy enough done, could happen to anyone," declared Shirley, bustling forward. "Come along, you two, we need you looking presentable for the big scene."

"Just five minutes!" Lynsey called out, but Shirley was already leading them to the old forge, and the supply of baby-wipes and tissues, kept in what she called her "clean-up box".

"It's at times like this I'd do anything for a coldwater tap around here," she commented, sorting out some old towels. "Good job you can get home to a nice, hot bath."

Oliver was already onstage, waiting for Scott's entrance:

> *Come, my good Edwin, and begin this task!*
> *For naught but horseshoes do my neighbours ask!*
> *These old charms, against doors they fix.*
> *To guard their metal from magic tricks!*

"Centre stage, Scott! Now, turn towards the forge — that's good — "

Scott obeyed Lynsey's stage instructions without thinking, his mind still on the girl with the plaited hair.

> *'Tis not the horseshoes that fill my mind.*
> *But a fair maiden, sweet and kind.*

Was the girl "sweet and kind"? The horse must think she was, thought Scott. But then, the horse hadn't been forced to put up with all the headaches she'd given Studio Workshop.

And yet — would he have stayed, all alone, in an old house which had been empty for years, with nobody to talk to, or lend a hand? Deep down, he doubted it. That girl had plenty of guts.

> *To make her mine, I'd see the race well run,*
> *Her troubles fade, with the setting of the sun . . .*

"Well done, Scott!" beamed Lynsey. "It was as if you were thinking about a real person, just then."

"Yes." Scott looked up at the sky, glad that he and Jason had decided to trust the girl, after all. "Yes, I suppose I was."

Jason, waiting for his cue as Lord Cuthbert, guessed how Scott was feeling. He had only managed to give a few garbled details between scenes to Oliver and the girls, and stunned surprise had quickly given way to suspicion, then excitement at the thought of finally learning the truth.

"I'd sooner have a real girl and a real, live horse, instead of something like a ghost," Tina said, which was exactly how each of them felt.

"Half term next week," Lynsey announced, at the end of rehearsals. "Let's see if we can get everyone word-perfect by Saturday."

Oliver watched her stuffing the scripts inside her case and trying to tidy her hair at the same time. He thought she seemed very tired. Feeling guilty, he said: "Sorry, Lyndsey. For all that bother with the security men earlier on, I mean."

"Security men?" She sighed, distractedly pushing her hair from her forehead. "Oh, that was just a storm in a tea cup, Oliver. If I here any more, maybe I'll ask Peter to step in. Doesn't look as if we're going to be here for much longer anyway, once the anniversary celebrations are over."

Oliver didn't know what to say. He'd tried not to think of leaving Dreyton Manor. It had become such a large part of their production. And yet, he supposed, it had always been a crazy idea that they might stay ... an old manor house, half-ruined ... Anyone could see it would cost a fortune to put everything right.

By the time everyone had gone home, the manor grounds felt so deserted that Jason and Scott began having doubts about seeing the girl or the black horse again.

It was Jason who heard the soft clip-clop of hooves across the grass, even before the girl appeared, leading the horse by a pair of makeshift reins.

She still looked tired and weepy, but she managed a weak sort of smile, as though she was pleased to see them.

"Hey, don't I know you?" exclaimed Rachel. "Isn't your name Gerda?"

"Not the stablegirl from Broad Oak?" cried Tina, remembering. "Charlie said you had to go home, because your father was ill."

"Yes, that's right," Gerda nodded wearily. "Look, let's get away from Dreyton Manor." Only Rachel noticed her looking up towards the grey, stone horse, and the fear in her brown eyes. "It's almost sunset. Domino and I usually walk along the footpath towards Broad Oak."

Domino seemed to enjoy all the attention she was getting. None of them could resist stroking her black coat or patting the side of her head, as Gerda led her along.

"I knew you'd like Domino," she smiled again. "Everyone does."

"All except people like Charlie who thinks she brings bad luck!" Tina reminded her.

"I was the one who started that rumour," Gerda sighed. "I had to think of some way to put people off finding out too much about us. That was the reason for the black cloak, as well."

She patted the bundle at the back of the shabby saddle, tucking a corner of black velvet out of sight.

"My father bought Domino cheaply as a foal, a weak little thing she was. But we worked hard, getting her fit, training her, and last year she began winning steeplechases. That was when the first owner wanted to buy her back."

"But why did you have to come to Dreyton Manor?" asked Oliver.

"Because we needed somewhere safe, where I could keep Domino while my father was in hospital. She kept being poorly, you see, and the last time we called the vet, he found traces of a sleeping draught in her food. There were only two of us looking after her, so we knew that somebody else had done it. But we didn't have any real proof."

"That's terrible!" cried Rachel indignantly. "Why should anyone want to do something like that?"

"Domino was beginning to be worth a lot of money," Gerda pointed out. "Enough to put our stables back in business. The year before, we'd been ready to sell up cheaply — before we entered Domino in her first race, that is."

"And who was going to buy the stables?" asked Oliver quietly.

"Major Foy. The man who sold us Domino."

It was all beginning to fit into place, slotting together like shapes in a pocket puzzle. A man planning to buy run-down stables at a bargain price. Then, a horse — a horse which he believed to be a weakling starting to make enough money for the business to thrive once again.

Take away the horse, Oliver mused, and the stables had nothing.

"Oh, if only I can keep Domino until the Merlin Television Handicap, next month. I know she would win easily. As well as the prize money, she'd be famous, so the Major wouldn't dare try any more tricks."

"You still haven't told us why you came to Dreyton Manor," Oliver reminded her. "Was it something to do with our Merrie Devil?"

"Yes." Gerda stared out into the deepening twilight. "Charlie mentioned it when I was at Broad Oak. But, I — I didn't really believe it was haunted ..."

"Haunted?" echoed Jason, the others glancing warily at each other. "But, the Whispering Chamber's only haunted in our play. And Scotty's worked all that out. You see — "

"No!" Gerda almost screamed. "No, that's what I thought when I read the script. But then, I — I hadn't seen John Gabriel, the Merrie Devil, and his lady appear. They come to the chamber almost every evening, just as the sun sets."

Seventeen

"What do you make of this ghost business, Ollie?" asked Scott, unwrapping batteries for his portable recorder.

"Gerda really believes it," Jason put in. "Why should she take Domino all the way up to Broad Oak every evening?"

"Yes, but look how scared we were about the horse noises that seemed to come from nowhere," Oliver reminded them. "And the strange sounds, the footsteps in the hall and everything else, but it's all been explained in the end!"

It was the sort of conversation they'd had before, whenever Gerda's name was mentioned.

"I — I know it sounds crazy," she had admitted. "That's what I thought. But John Gabriel really is there every evening, wearing the same sort of jerkin and shirt that's in the Castle Museum. Tall, he is, with a light brown beard and moustache. And his lady has long, fair hair. A bit like yours," she added, nodding at Rachel.

The three boys remembered it all as they packed up the microphones and cassette tapes after they had recorded a series of spooky sound effects in the Whispering Chamber.

The result was a jumble of mad, cackling laughter and evil chuckles that was certain to spook the audience.

Now Scott was ready to try the sound effects out during a rehearsal. Backstage, Robert and Daniel were draping the mirrors lining the walls of the garden room with as many lengths of black material as they could find, ready for the demons in their black leotards to leap out of the darkness, accompanied by the moans and groans on the cassette recorder.

Scott's fingers hovered over the push-buttons, the volume control set as high as it would go. He was watching the stage intently, waiting for the demons to appear, his cue to start the tape.

The sound effects were perfect, even Lynsey was enthusiastic. "Why not have Jason speaking and crying out like Oliver did, then playing it back on the tape?" Lynsey suggested. "He could sound just as tormented as he's acting, then."

Oliver and Jason beamed at each other, and Scott's green eyes sparkled, all thinking the same thing. Another visit to the Whispering Chamber.

"Maybe we'll get the ghost, next time," grinned Oliver, rubbing his hands.

Later on, he would say that it had only been a joke. But Jason and Scott were so pleased with the success of the sound effects, and so full of daring at the thought of knowing their way around the Whispering Chamber, that they nodded at once.

"So, we meet back here at sunset, right?" said Scott, dropping his voice to a whisper.

The light had begun to change by the time they crept into the Whispering Chamber. Three pairs of eyes watched a smoky, yellow glow creeping across the walls, the air cold enough to make the boys shiver.

"Th-this is it," gulped Oliver, clenching his fists in an effort to stop himself shaking. "Here he comes."

They were powerless to move, seeing their own frightened reflections in the long line of mirrors, exploding in a silver flash of light.

"Keep looking!" commanded Oliver, between clenched teeth. "Keep looking!"

There came another flash, bright enough to show every corner of the enormous room, like a photograph in an old, forgotten album. Then, a sinister rumble booming through the walls, louder and louder, until it seemed to crash right down on the very spot where the boys stood, huddled together.

"Look!" shrieked Scott, frantically nodding towards the balcony window. "Some — somebody's trying to get in!"

The window was being pushed from the outside, as if some big, heavy shoulder was heaving against it. One jagged white flash after another shot through the crack. The great room flickered and trembled, before another crash, even louder this time, threw them to the floor, an army of footsteps scurrying towards them.

A moment's silence. Then, a vicious-sounding wail weaved its way in through the window, sending a spatter of wet leaves and bits of nest gusting towards the terrified boys, clutching at Oliver's hair and showering Jason's glasses.

"Rain," he murmured dazedly, feeling one lens with his fingers. "It — it's raining, outside."

None of the three boys had ever been frightened of thunderstorms. But they were all glad to see the lightning becoming more and more dim as each roll of thunder moved further away.

Gradually, the rain became a soft patter, the wind nothing more than a breeze stirring the damp cobwebs hanging above their heads.

"And no Merrie Devil," sighed Oliver at last, putting into words what the other two felt — a strange mixture of relief and disappointment.

"So it looks as if you were right, Ollie," added Scott, with another shiver. "Gerda must've been imagining things, just like we did."

"Can't blame her, though. Every time there was a flash of lightning, I was sure John Gabriel was about to appear, standing right in front of us!"

"Or kicking his way through the balcony window," finished Jason soberly.

"Come on," said Oliver. "Time we were getting home!"

Everyone took great care not to mention the ghost after that. Tina took one look at Scott's face, so pale that every freckle seemed to stand out on its own, with smudges of soot around his eyes and in his hair, and said nothing.

Oliver's father was out playing bridge with Jason's dad by the time he got home. And, as his mother was holding a meeting of the Woman's Guild in the lounge, there was no need for any explanations.

They chose to forget all that Gerda had told them. Only when Oliver put on his blacksmith's beard and began the speech, "'The sun puts his head on his pillow, the ocean . . .'" did Jason and Scott glance at each other with a special look of understanding.

Gerda no longer referred to the Merrie Devil either, except when they were talking about the Studio Workshop production, watching Scott and Jason fixing the scenery, or Oliver finishing off the posters.

Her favourite was one which Rachel had designed, with the black silhouette of a horse's head at each corner.

"Might almost be Domino," she smiled, tracing the outline lovingly. "Makes me wish I could stay to see the final performance."

This was news to Tina and Rachel, and Gerda had to chuckle at the surprise on their faces.

"Got to go home to finish training Domino for the Merlin Television Handicap," she explained. "Dad says it's only a matter of another ten days or so before he comes out of hospital."

"That's fantastic, Gerda!" cried Rachel. "You deserve something nice to happen."

"So do you. And at least I'll still be here for the full dress rehearsal. Everyone seems to be talking about *The Merrie Devil of Dreyton, or The Whispering Chamber*!"

Rachel laughed, and Tina rubbed Domino's long nose the way she liked it, both trying not to appear too flattered by all the attention that Studio Workshop was suddenly getting.

"FORGOTTEN MANUSCRIPT UNEARTHED BY YOUTH DRAMA GROUP," the *Dreyton Gazette* had proclaimed to its readers, once details of the Anniversary Celebrations had been announced. "FIRST PUBLIC PERFORMANCE SINCE 1839!"

"Cripes!" had been Oliver's first comment, when Lynsey showed them the report. "Let's hope the production isn't a big let-down, after this."

"Why say that, Oliver? I told you *The Merrie Devil* would attract a lot of interest, didn't I?"

"Yes, but supposing it's a big flop, and nobody likes it?" wailed Tina. "We'll be a laughing stock after this build-up!"

"*Nobody's* going to be a laughing stock!" Lynsey insisted, suddenly grim. "Now, listen. You've worked hard on this production. And we're going to see that it's a success, if only to show that we're not giving up without a fight."

"What do you mean, Lynsey?" Oliver asked. "Studio Workshop's not giving anything up, are we?"

They waited anxiously, watching Lynsey clutching at her hair as she answered.

"Well ... we can't possibly run Dreyton Manor by ourselves once winter's here, and we need lighting and heating. And the council certainly don't have the money to put everything right."

"We've still got the Parish Hall," said Rachel comfortingly.

"Yes, but that's booked almost every Saturday. Besides, the hire charges are going up again, and we don't have anywhere to store our stuff. It's a losing battle, trying to manage."

116

Nobody knew what to say. Staying at Dreyton Manor was, they knew, little more than a dream. But the dream was far, far better than being squeezed out of the Parish Hall, with nowhere else to go.

When *The Merrie Devil of Dreyton* was finished, it could easily be the end of them, too.

"After all our hard work," said Rachel, leafing dismally through the collection of posters she had just picked up. "It doesn't seem fair."

"It isn't fair!" Oliver burst out, making them all jump. "But at least *The Merrie Devil of Dreyton* gives us a chance. Does the *Dreyton Gazette* know this might be our last production? If that doesn't get us a big audience, on top of everything else, nothing will! Studio Workshop gets all the money from the tickets and the programmes this time, don't forget."

"Enough to keep us going for a bit longer?" Scott queried, turning to Lynsey.

"Yes, I would think so. And if things went really well, we might even start a fund, or something. You never know."

"Worth a try," commented Jason.

"Nothing to lose, anyway," added Rachel, watching a slow smile spread across Lynsey's pretty face.

"Thanks for cheering me up. Now, let's have another look at these fantastic posters of yours."

Dreyton Manor began to look different, too — still a half-ruined, old country mansion, but now with plywood and hardboard gradually being tidied up, and bits of rubbish cleared away.

The worst job of all was hacking down the overgrown grass to make a lawn where the audience could sit. Scott's dad had been pleased to lend an old-fashioned push-along mower. But it was hard work, clearing just a small strip at a time.

117

"Shame Domino couldn't have kept it a bit shorter," Gerda teased, feeding the horse with mints at the end of one particularly hot and sticky Sunday afternoon. "I've never been able to let her graze too often in this part of the manor."

"What about after we've gone home?" Scott suggested at once, grimly surveying a collection of blisters on his hands. "That would help!" Then he remembered. "Not still bothered about the ghost of the Merrie Devil, are you? We've already said, we waited and waited for him to appear, and nothing happened! Well," he added, remembering the thunderstorm, "nothing happened about the ghost, anyway."

"I was thinking about the extra rehearsals and more people coming here," replied Gerda, in a cold voice. "And, as for the the ghost, you can believe and say whatever you like, Scott."

"Look, Scott didn't mean to upset you, Gerda," Tina began, trying to stop her leading Domino away. She hated any kind of unpleasantness. "Don't let him spoil the rest of the time we've still got together."

Scott opened his mouth to defend himself, but Jason cut in first.

"He was only trying to put her mind at rest, Tina. We were stuck inside the Whispering Chamber until well past sunset."

"You couldn't have been," said Gerda. "There wasn't any sunset."

"You are talking about the last rehearsal at half-term, aren't you?" Tina continued, looking from one indignant face to the other. "When you left Rachel and me to come home on our own, and it started pouring with rain? Well, there wasn't any sunset."

"'Course there was a sunset!" Scott snapped at her,

118

annoyed to think that everyone was paying so much attention to what his little sister said. "The sun rises and sets every day,"

"'The sun rests his head on his pillow, the ocean,'" Oliver quoted from *The Merrie Devil*.

"Not that night, it didn't!" Tina retorted, in a flash of anger. "I should know! I was looking out for my golden horse!"

Scott gave a loud groan. "I might have known that flipping golden horse was behind all this! Wouldn't surprise me if you blew the thing a goodnight kiss when you shut yourself in your room every night!"

Red-faced, Tina turned away. Once Scott had made up his mind about something, she knew that he hated to think he could be wrong. And it wasn't as if the ghost of the Merrie Devil was really important to them, she told herself miserably.

Or, was it?

Wasn't their production called *The Merrie Devil of Dreyton, or The Whispering Chamber*? And wasn't she playing the part of Firefly, pretending to haunt the Whispering Chamber on the orders of John Gabriel, the blacksmith?

"D-don't go away, Gerda!" Tina yelled at the top of her voice. "Not just yet! Wait till I get back from the Whispering Chamber!"

"What?" Scott cried out in alarm, knowing she had only ventured into the enormous, dark room once before. "Tina, don't be daft! You haven't even got a torch!"

Tina pretended not to hear, stumbling her way through the forge and up into the passage, feeling around the smooth, tiled walls to guide herself along.

The three boys soon caught up with her, but not before she had scrambled into the chamber, her eyes already on a thin finger of sunlight which was slowly billowing out like a huge flower.

This time, Jason noticed that their reflections seemed to fade quickly into a thin, white haze, before darkening into deep pools of shadow.

"Now ..." whispered Gerda, coming up behind Jason. "Now!"

On one side of the room, a bright, golden glow began beaming down, like a giant spotlight on to the centre of a stage. The light glinted and sparkled on a strange, silver mist, melting into the shape of tall, black boots. Then, the breeches, the jerkin, the full-sleeved shirt, the handsome, tanned face, the curling beard and moustache, and the head of the stone horse, looking over his shoulder.

The Merrie Devil was exactly as Gerda had described, holding the hand of a beautiful young lady in a tunic dress, with flowers in her long, fair hair.

Eighteen

The Merrie Devil stood quite still, his clear blue eyes staring out at them.

Everything about him had a dazzling glow — his face, the colours of the clothes he wore, the shine on his boots.

Almost like a piece of scenery, Scott thought crazily.

It seemed they watched for a long, long time, until first the horse began melting into the silver mist background, then the edges of the lady's tunic dress and her long hair, John Gabriel's boots, his jerkin and shirt... all fading, piece by piece, until his eyes looked out for the last time and merged into the dim sheen of the mirror.

They stood together in silence for some time, none of them daring to move until the light had mellowed, bathing the walls with a soft, cream sheen.

"I — I don't believe it," breathed Oliver at last, his heart still thumping. "It — it's impossible!"

"I know how you feel," Gerda replied. "That's what I kept telling myself at first."

"But, why does he appear at this time?" Jason wondered, surprised to find himself speaking quite calmly. "And only when there's a proper sunset?"

Scott had his arm around Tina, who was trying hard not to burst into tears.

She was the one who kept her eyes open, he scolded himself, and he had been the last one to listen. Yet, she had proved that when the golden horse shone in the sky, so the Merrie Devil appeared.

"Let's get outside again," Rachel pleaded, backing away nervously. "P-please, let's get out of here."

"But there's nothing here, now," Scott said slowly. He paused, thinking hard and looking all around. "Remember how we thought ghosts were looking at us, and it turned out to be our own reflections?"

"But, there's nothing on this wall where we saw the Merrie Devil that would show in the mirror," said Jason, glancing over his shoulder, just to make sure. "Look how dusty everything is. The colours would never have come out as bright as we saw them."

"Like a scenery back-drop," remembered Scott. "Except that the mirror's all blotchy."

"Nearly all the mirrors on that side are like that," said Gerda. "That's where the light's best, yet none of them are much better than the one I broke."

"And that had the silvering worn away from the back," Oliver recalled, edging closer to the ornate frame with growing interest. "Just the same as this one, with great patches of plain glass."

"What?" Scott almost choked out. "Jason, let's get the balcony window open a bit further! Tina and Rachet, give us a hand!"

The window had not been opened properly for so long that the bottom edge had sagged down and made a deep groove in the floor of the balcony. It took a lot of pushing and shoving to wedge it open just a few inches but that was enough.

"It *is* mostly clear glass, Ollie! See anything through it?"

"Nothing much ... Only blackness ... "

"Keep going," yelled Scott, thumping a fist against his other hand. "I bet you'll find it changing to dark blue, the higher you get up the mirror!"

"Hey! You're right! How did you know?"

"That's the colour of John Gabriel's trousers," squealed Tina. "We can see nearly all of him, now. And the horse! And the lady!"

122

"Stand back a bit, then you'll see, as well," Rachel cried out eagerly. "It's a picture! A huge, great picture, hidden behind that mirror for years and years and years."

"I'll go and fetch my dad," Oliver decided quickly. "You come with me, Jason, and the girls can stay back here with Scotty."

Mr Davis wasn't too pleased at having his Sunday afternoon interrupted, especially by two wild-eyed boys gabbling about ghosts and devils and forgotten paintings behind mirrors.

"I'm warning you, Oliver," he said at last, reaching for his wallet and car keys, "if this is some kind of joke ..."

But the rest of the sentence was left unspoken. Even without the earnest pleading in Oliver's eyes and the desperation in his voice, he knew when his son was being serious.

It was Jason's idea to pick Lynsey up on the way, and very soon they were being led up the passage and into the Whispering Chamber – this time with plenty of torches and hurricane lamps which Oliver's dad had insisted on bringing, sending yellow pools of light wavering towards Scott and the girls.

"It's like being in a dream," Lynsey kept saying, all the time the mirror was being examined with magnifying glasses and special lenses.

"Definitely something valuable there," Oliver's dad announced at last. "And behind the rest of these mirrors, too, I shouldn't wonder. This one's signed by a famous artist called Bramley, and he usually painted a series of pictures. It's about two hundred years old and valuable too, unless I'm very much mistaken."

There was no mistake. Experts were called in next day and Oliver felt very proud of his father when, one by one, the mirrors were removed to reveal the line of paintings, and all by Charles Bramley, just as he had said.

"The stonework had crumbled away such a lot over the years that the sun could shine right through to the back of the Merrie Devil painting," Lynsey explained. "So, as the mirror silvering gradually wore away, more and more of the painting could be seen through the glass."

"So, the Merrie Devil stayed at Dreyton Manor," said Tina softly, smiling up at the handsome, tanned face. "And his lady. Was she really the squire's daughter?"

"Yes," nodded the man from the museum, "she was. But the story of Lady Elizabeth Melrose falling in love with her father's blacksmith — so much so, that she had many little monuments built for him — was always thought to be a legend. All anyone knew was that she died as a young woman, and the estate passed to a distant cousin."

"And John Gabriel?" asked Rachel huskily. "What happened to him?"

"Well, he would have left Dreyton Manor. The idea of a noble lady marrying a blacksmith would have been thought of as a real disgrace. That's probably the reason why the pictures were hidden behind those hideous mirrors."

Once the news about the Bramley collection of long-lost paintings was announced, a great many people wanted to come and see Dreyton Manor. Nearly every one of the remaining rehearsals was attended by newspaper reporters, and interviewers from magazines, radio stations, and even television, all anxious to talk to Oliver, Scott, Jason, Tina and Rachel, and to hear about the Merrie Devil. And each time, Studio Workshop were asked to perform an extract from *The Merrie Devil of Dreyton, or The Whispering Chamber*!

"Marvellous practice for the final production!" Lynsey kept saying, after every shower of congratulations. "We'll have the biggest audience in the whole of the Anniversary Celebrations!"

The only sad part was having to say goodbye to Gerda and Domino. Rachel and Tina had become very fond of both of them, and it was hard for all three girls not to feel tearful when the time came for Gerda to leave.

"You ought to be here with us, sharing in all the excitement," said Rachel, giving Domino one last pat. "You were the one who told us about the Merrie Devil being in the Whispering Chamber."

"You probably would have stumbled across it, sooner or later," smiled Gerda.

"Just make sure Domino wins the Merlin Television Handicap," Oliver told her. "Same day as our production, isn't it?"

"That's right!" Gerda swung herself easily into the saddle, her riding hat set firmly on her head. "All our training so far has been done after dark, so this last stretch should be a real doddle. Only a visit to the blacksmith at Willoughby, and we're on our way."

"We'll see Charlie gets his tools back," Rachel promised solemnly.

"Shame the Merrie Devil isn't here," added Jason, trying to cheer them up.

"But, he *is* here," said Tina, with a glance at the stone horse. "He's been here, the whole time."

Something else was happening on the day of Studio Workshop's performance of *The Merrie Devil*. It was Peter Albany-Smith who told them about the Charles Bramley paintings going on display at a famous Art Gallery, before being auctioned at the end of the month.

"So many art dealers and collectors will be bidding for them," he declared grandly. "I shouldn't be surprised if you become almost as famous as I am!"

Luckily, they were saved the embarrassment of thinking up a polite reply, because Albany-Smith noticed the Mayor of Dreyton's car purring towards the back gates of the manor.

"Quite an audience we're getting this afternoon, don't you think, Alan? Such a pity we haven't had time to find some flags or fairy lights, like the wonderful array at the Civic Centre and along the High Street."

"Flags and fairy lights? At Dreyton Manor?" snorted Jason, viewing the grey walls and tall chimneys. "Talk about having half–baked ideas."

"Wait till he sees our demons and hears all the creepy wails from the Whispering Chamber," grinned Scott. "He'll get a whole lot more than fairy lights!"

"As long as the first performance goes all right," commented Oliver guardedly, watching still more seats being carried onto the lawn. Everyone who had seen extracts of the play had seemed impressed, he told himself, fixing his beard with a hand which he was annoyed to find trembled slightly.

But suppose the sight of such a huge audience made everyone forget their lines? Suppose Shirley didn't come in with the right prompt, or the scenery fell down, or Scotty's tape recorder didn't work, or, or . . .

Suzy started the play, her voice sounding so clear that the last murmurs from the audience instantly died away.

Oliver squared his shoulders and put the finishing touches to his beard, the chorus of delighted cries which greeted the arrival of so many favourite nursery rhyme characters making him smile.

No Studio Workshop production had ever been so popular. There were sighs for Edwin and the beautiful Mathilda. Boos and hisses for the villain, Lord Cuthbert. Squeals and shrieks at the arrival of Firefly and all the little demons.

When the ghosts appeared, Scott turned up the volume

as high as he dared, hoping to see Albany-Smith fall off his chair. It was something of a let-down when he only jerked back in his seat — although the Mayor did drop his programme, then got his chain tangled up trying to retrieve it, which went some way to make up for the disappointment.

What cheers and applause greeted the brave Edwin, taking the hand of Mathilda on their wedding day, with all the country folk of Dreyton celebrating and bringing them the gifts they had made.

And it was only when the Mayor of Dreyton stepped up on to the stage and held up his hands for silence that the audience finally ceased clapping Oliver's performance as John Gabriel.

"Ladies and gentlemen! I am sure you would like to join me in congratulating Studio Workshop on an excellent first production of *The Merrie Devil of Dreyton*! A play which, I am sure, many people will look forward to seeing and to performing in the future."

"Hear, hear!" shouted someone, and the clapping began again, so loudly that it was some time before the Mayor could continue.

"As you will all know by now, this production has led to the discovery of some valuable art treasures. It has been decided that most of the money raised from the sale of the Charles Bramley paintings will go towards the renovation of Dreyton Manor, so that it may become an Arts Centre for groups such as Studio Workshop."

"We can stay!" cried Tina, giving Rachel a hug backstage. "We're staying at Dreyton Manor, along with the Merrie Devil!"

"Two more things to announce!" the Mayor was bellowing, above the cheers and cries of approval. "A telephone message which was passed to me at the interval, to say that Domino has won the Merlin Television Handicap. I hope that's good news for somebody here."

"And," he continued, not seeming to notice more hugs and smiles from the side of the stage, "as well as today being the start of Dreyton's Six Hundredth Anniversary Celebrations, it also happens to be the twenty-first birthday of Studio Workshop's producer, Miss Lynsey Ronald!"

"Lynsey's birthday!" gasped Rachel, as the crowds began singing "*Happy Birthday To You*." "We didn't do anything about Lynsey's birthday!"

"Don't you believe it, Rachel," smiled Lynsey happily. "Anyone can go into a shop and buy something. But you've given me your time, your thought, and a lovely day to remember. And that's the best birthday present I've ever had!"

"A wonderful performance, young lady!" the Mayor of Dreyton had begun. "And, may I say ... "

A surprised hush descended on the audience as they waited for him to continue, but he had lifted his eyes towards the magnificent head, the mane and the stone hooves raised up to the sky.

"I'm so very sorry," he apologized at last, stroking his forehead. "But it it's really quite extraordinary. For a moment, I could swear I heard the sound of a horse whinnying."